Going Back

Going Back

stories

Tony Richards

LASTIC
PRESS

To the memory of Dave Stirzaker, champion of causes, larger-than-life character, and fishing buddy.

Table of contents

Going Back

After it happened, my marriage only lasted two more months. Janine? She would tell me, some fifty times a day, that it wasn't really my fault. But she never looked in my eyes once, each time she said it. And by mid-February, she was gone.

My drinking, already bad, went into overdrive at that point. My good job and my nice home went the same way as my marriage. Family and friends all tried their best, but ended up abandoning me. Only one thing, in the end, prevented me from going all the way down. It was that ... however low I seemed to sink, however much I tried to deaden the pain with alcohol ... every single time I closed my eyes, I could still see it, hear it. Josie stepping off the kerb into the traffic. The squeal of tyres on frozen asphalt. And a small, truncated shriek.

It was what pulled me together finally. I realised that I only had two choices. Kill myself. Or try to stop it, try to save her.

That meant going back.

Modern science was no use to me at all in that endeavour, so I turned to older belief systems, starting with the local ones first. Wikka, and then Druidism. I studied them back to front, spent time with their practitioners. Eventually discovered there was nothing for me there, and so I went to the Americas, starting in New Mexico and travelling ever south.

Mushrooms were ingested, powders sniffed, potions swallowed, smoke inhaled. I painted my face, danced and chanted. And a dozen times during that period, I did go back, grab Josie just in time, and everything would be all right again. And then, some two or three days later, I would slowly come around. Realise that only my dreams had been altered. Nothing more.

Finally, like thousands of searchers after greater truths before me, I decided to go East.

In Japan, I found him. Half an hour's slow train ride outside Kyoto, there is Nara, a most holy place, by virtue of its sacred Deer Park. It has almost as many shrines as roving, half-tame deer.

I went to the largest building first, the hulking, dim Daibutsuden. Spent almost an hour wandering around it, under the impassive gaze of the vast, shadow-clad bronze figure of Buddha which dominated the whole place. Found nothing of use there. When I emerged, I consulted my map. And discovered that there was another, equally important site some twenty minutes' walk away, across the park from there. Actually amongst the woods. The Kasuga Taisha Shrine.

Right there in the trees. And animism, connection with nature – I had already concluded – was pretty important, if I was ever going to find my way back. I could only travel backwards to the point where I saved Josie if the world allowed me to. It was a matter of ... receiving its permission.

It was well gone midday by this time. It had rained heavily all the previous night, and the sky was still so filled with black pendulous cloud that I moved through an early twilight. I was alone as I walked across the open grassland to the trees. The few tourists who'd arrived today were still clustered around the temples. As I went in through the branches, down the narrow track, the light became still dimmer. By the time I reached the shrine, I could barely see ahead of me at all. Until I reached it.

The place was especially wondrous in semi-darkness. There amongst the wood were ranked thousands of stone and metal lanterns. Only a few of them were lit, so that the rest looked only half-real. There was silence all around me, save for the occasional drip of water from the tall, rain-sodden trees. I could have stayed there until true night fell, so wrapped up was I in it all.

When the priest stepped out from nowhere, I ought to have been startled. But he did it in so gentle and so delicate a way that I was not alarmed at all. He seemed to be tall and thin, though I could not be quite certain of that. He was dressed from head to toe in dark grey robes, so that his frame was barely visible at all, his face seemed to float quite unsupported in the dimness. A young face, the scalp clean-shaven. Eyebrows gone, and high cheekbones, and lips so full and curved that I could almost have been looking at a girl. He gazed at me for a few seconds, expression impassive, only his eyes smiling at the sight of me. And then he beckoned me to follow him.

I had done stranger things than this by far, the last few years. And so I followed without question.

Further back in the woods was a small stone hut, the door lit by a single candle. This he disappeared inside, to re-emerge from seconds later with something clasped in his fist. He didn't show me what it was, at first. Just stared at me again, as though waiting.

And I don't know what did it, but it all came pouring out.

Out shopping with Josie ... just before Christmas ... frost on the paving stones, breath misting on the air ... she just four years old, so excited ... and I kept hold of her hand the whole time, yes I did, I promise I did, except ... except ... the old woman passing by us, losing her footing on a patch of ice ... and I reaching across to steady her out of pure instinct ...

"I only let go of Josie's hand for a few seconds!" I was now crying out loud, amongst the darkened trees. "A few seconds, oh God, I swear it!"

The priest, his eyes still smiling, reached out with the index finger of his free hand. Let one of my tears drip onto it. Then clasped that in his palm as well, as though it were some gem.

He showed me what he had fetched from the hut.

It was no bigger than an old penny. A tiny disc of metal, of a greenish hue. And ranked around its outer rim were twelve evenly-spaced Japanese characters. Like a clock, but with no mechanism and no hands.

He gave it to me.

"You must return to where it happened, the exact same place," he told me.

His lips were not moving in any kind of rhythm to the words that I was listening to. Was he speaking in his own tongue, and I hearing in mine?

"You must hold this in both hands, and think about what happened. And then, you can go back. You can put it right."

"But," he warned me, with a sympathetic sternness, "there will be a price."

Really? And could it be any worse than the prices I'd already paid? I nodded my thanks to him, and then started back for England.

*

It was even the precise same date. Four years to the day since Josie had run off into the traffic. I waited till gone midnight, when the high street would be empty. Then I returned to the exact spot.

Four years since I'd been here, but it was easy to find.

I clasped the little disc between my palms, in a prayer attitude. And closed my eyes. And remembered the squeal of tyres, the brief shriek. They were still there, fresh as ever in my skull.

And when I opened my eyes, it was daylight, the street around me was full of people. There was the old lady, slipping on the patch of ice.

Someone else reached out to catch her anyway.

I swung sharply to my right. And there she was.

A frozen moment...

In which, I could even see what she had been running towards. Over on the far side of the street, a woman was walking, on a pair of tartan leashes, a brace of West Highland terrier pups, so young that they looked no more than animated balls of fluff. And Josie had loved puppies – I had promised her one when she was old enough to look after it, such a hollow promise now.

Her whole tiny body was straining towards the little pups, both of her arms outstretched.

One of her feet had already left the kerb.

The frozen moment passed. I lunged forwards. And grabbed her by the fleece-lined hood of her smart winter coat. And dragged her back.

I'd done it. So I hugged her. But she simply struggled in my arms, let out a troubled whimper.

That was when a hand descended on my shoulder, from behind.

*

"Christ almighty, thank you," said a voice.

And my insides seemed to tighten. Because that voice – it seemed rather too familiar.

"I only let go of her for a moment," the man behind me was now saying. "I don't know what I was thinking of."

Then he reached down, and scooped Josie out of my helpless grasp.

Slowly, I straightened. Turned around. Looked at him.

This wasn't what I had envisaged, all this time I'd dreamt of going back. I had meant to return to the same place and same time, the way I'd been. And put everything right. And go on with my life the way it had supposed to be.

Instead of which...?

I was looking at Me.

And the strangest thing of all was that he didn't even seem to recognise me.

Strangest thing. Until I caught sight of my own reflection just behind him, in the glaze of a shop window.

I and Me? Just four years apart, we were completely different. He, clean cut and clean-shaven, conventionally dressed, sporty-looking, with his skin pale from the drizzly English weather.

And myself? I had a beard now, and my hair grew down across my shoulders. My skin was baked brown from years spent in far warmer climes, and my clothing was a rag-bag collection from half across the world.

And yet ... it wasn't even this that truly separated us.

I looked at his face and his eyes, unaltered by experience, untouched by hardship, tragedy.

Then I stared, very hard, at the reflected sight of mine.

We might as well have come from different planets.

He was looking at me strangely now, as though suspecting that there might be something wrong with me, wrong in the head. But then his politeness took over, and he thanked me once again. He even wished me Merry Christmas before going on his way.

I watched me bobbing off along the high street, with my daughter clasped tight in my arms. Watched me heading back towards my nice home and my loving wife. My good job and my promising, unblemished future.

One that I would never know.

At least I'd saved her. There was consolation, plenty of it, just in that.

I waited till I'd disappeared completely, before going on my way.

A Place In The Country

She awoke in her tiny apartment, just before the next day's dawn, to a mild hangover, an awful soreness in her eyes from crying. And a horrible tiredness, one that was far more than simply physical. Lying fully-clothed on top of her bedsheets, in a dress all damp and crumpled.

It was always cold past summer, in her dingy, cramped bedroom behind Prospect Place. The sun didn't get in here, ever. And the hot water pipes were off until mid-October. Grace Tilling had never found the courage to complain.

Awkwardly, she got up from the bed, went to her window with its rusting fire escape framing the view beyond. Trash cans were picked out in the eerie pre-dawn light – 'the scenic view', she sometimes called it. She had almost no savings. Worked at a little travel agency four blocks away, taking bookings over the phone and tapping at a computer. And she was thirty five, and would be thirty six in two months time.

Now, she realised, the view from her window might never be improved. Her dream of a place in the countryside? It had been ripped from her grasp.

It wasn't the reason she'd loved him, but Jay'd had money. They had talked about moving away from Brooklyn. To New Hampshire maybe. Or Vermont. Some place where the sky could be seen the entire time. Somewhere calm and peaceful, clean.

All of that had just been talk, though. Just a wistful dream. He'd dumped her, last night. He'd been using her. He'd just seen her as something fun.

Grace shivered and turned away, reaching for her robe, which was lying in a heap on the floor. As she picked it up, a cockroach scuttled from beneath it. *Damn this place!*

The city was starting to come alive around her, by this time. The hum of traffic steadily rose. A radio came on, loudly, in a neighbouring apartment. Someone started shouting at somebody else.

It all ... ground at her. Wormed into her. Set her teeth on edge.

Stiffly, trying to ignore it, Grace went off into the bathroom, to prepare herself for work.

*

It came to her at lunchtime, in the diner she frequented round the corner from the agency. And it arrived – as ideas sometimes do – completely and utterly from out of the blue.

Out of *less* than blue. From nothing.

There was a couple seated at the table behind hers. And they were discussing how to decorate their home.

The thought suddenly lighted in her head, making her whole face stiffen. The movement of her fork stopped. More, she practically dropped the thing.

She turned the notion over. It seemed utterly insane, at first.

But ... no. It might just work.

If she couldn't move out to the countryside ... *then why not bring it here?*

That image bloomed inside her, growing denser, taking proper shape, the entire afternoon. But the biggest problem...?

Her plan didn't need an awful lot of money, but it needed *some*. And where could she get it?

*

How the agency survived at all, she had no idea. The owner, Mr. Frankelman, was nearing his seventies, and had certain very fixed ideas around the concept of vacations. Certain notions about reliability and quality that were as out-of-date as his own dress-sense. There was a list of airlines on her desk which were the only ones she was allowed to book from – TWA was still on it, for God's sake! And another list for hotel chains. She knew that she could do much better for less cash. Little wonder that business had flagged so much she hadn't even got a raise this year.

The next morning was pretty typical. Mr. Coombes, from Trenton, had just taken early-retirement, a fat pay-off cheque. And wanted to go with his wife and his four teenaged kids on a long-dreamt-of tour of Europe. He gave her the destinations. She worked out the figures for him.

"Jesus Christ, that much?" he muttered. "I'd no idea that it was going to be that much!"

It came to Grace instantly what she could do. She looked around quickly to make sure no one was listening, then said, "Let me have your number, Mr. Coombes. I'll see if I can get back to you later on with something better."

She spent the next hour on the Internet, inspecting sites that Mr. Frankelman would never have approved of.

Dialled the number she'd been given as soon as she got in through her front door.

"Mr. Coombes?" Her heart was pounding. She was praying that he'd not already found a better deal. "I see Madrid's on your itinerary. Would you object to starting there instead of London? Good. Well if you take an internal flight to Miami in the first place – "

"What?"

She pressed on quickly. "Iberia have an excellent group offer all this month. Even including the cost of the internal tickets and an overnight at an airport hotel, you can save yourself $180 per person on the return trans-Atlantic flight. That's a total of – "

"I *know* what that's a total of." Mr. Coombes sounded half-impressed and half-puzzled. "Why didn't you tell me this before?"

Grace went on to explain how, with different but equally good hotels to the ones she'd first suggested, and by making use of the excellent one-way fares the newer budget European carriers offered, he could save himself a further eighteen to nineteen hundred easily.

"There'd be a booking fee for this of ..." And she took a deep breath, and then said, "Seventy dollars?"

"When you've just saved me three thousand bucks?" Mr. Coombes asked her, almost sarcastically. "It's a deal."

She let the breath out again when she put the phone down a minute later. Squeezed her eyes tight shut. She'd done it!

And it worked again two days later. And again the next day after that. By the end of the month, she'd saved enough to buy her own computer.

Then she started fleshing out her dream.

*

The first thing to be dealt with, obviously, was the noise. The constant, insensate growling of the city, and the bedlam from her neighbours. During the next few weeks, she bought stacks of acoustic panelling and tiles. She put floor insulation under the linoleum. It whittled down the size still further of her already cramped home, but she considered that a small price to be paid.

The windows were the *real* problem, since she was not allowed – and, besides, could not afford – to knock the frames out. She settled for secondary glazing, hauling and then cutting to size heavy sheets of glass.

Some thin noises still came in by the time she was finished. But ... when she put a record on, they vanished. So her home was filled with music from then, all the time she was indoors.

She had to settle for imitation oak panelling, far less expensive than the real thing. Retrieved a small carved ceiling beam from a skip. The rugs came from a clearance sale. The imitation coal fire was bought second-hand. And most of the furniture – dressers, and a rocking chair – she picked up by searching tirelessly through every rummage sale and every last thrift shop.

Her place in the country was almost complete. Only the view was left.

Grace swung open the new windowpanes she'd fitted. And she glued, to the original glass, photographs that she'd had printed to the exact size. Photographs from the kind of magazines that had always fuelled her original ambition. Country scenes.

Once it was done, she could look at, from her living room, a massive open green space that was dotted with wild flowers. A broad and grassy vista that swept off beneath a clear blue sky towards a row of distant hills.

And from her bedroom? A distant, white-painted wooden church. And a sparkling brook. And woodlands. Might deer live in them?

A police siren went by on Prospect, and she could still hear it very faintly. That annoyed her. Grace went over to her stereo, and carefully unsleeved the record she had bought for this occasion. Beethoven's Symphony No. 6 in F – the 'Pastoral'.

And, as its soft melody filled up her apartment, the music swallowed every last bit of encroaching noise. Grace calmed down now, smiled.

The city beyond her walls?

It no longer existed.

*

A year from starting all this, she was finally able to quit her job. Not a moment too soon – even Mr. Frankelman was starting to notice that trade had become unnaturally slow. By that time, she had her own website set up, the Mr. Coombes' of the world were fetching her new business by word of mouth. And she walked out of the door with a list of all the agency's regular clients – what time of year they vacationed, where, and at what price – folded up in her purse.

Had anything ever stopped her from doing this before? No, nothing, she acknowledged, feeling rather stupid at the thought. She simply hadn't been so driven, until this point. Had never had a definite, achievable goal to claw towards.

It occurred to her every so often – now that she was no longer physically tied to the city – why shouldn't she actually move out? But again, no. She'd worked so very long and hard to fashion this place to her vision. And she wasn't going anywhere.

She almost never ventured outside these days. And when she occasionally did so, it was with the sense of 'visiting the city'. Her groceries were delivered to her door. That, and most everything else, could be dealt with through the Net.

Her few friends phoned from time to time. But she kept on giving them excuses, till the calls gradually trailed away.

Everything was as she wanted it to be, now. Everything was perfect. All she wished to do was stay in her place in the country, living out her dream. Month, after month, and then more of them.

Just how many of them had there been by this time? Ten? She checked her diary. Fourteen.

Every once in a while – looking up from her keyboard – she might believe, these days, that she'd just seen a bird whisking across the clear blue sky beyond her front window.

And, lying in her bed some nights, her drapes still wide open, she was sure that she could hear a low wind humming by. Did it make the church bell clatter faintly? Did it make the woodlands move?

That bothered her, at first. Didn't seem natural or right.

But her unease lessened, as the months continued to overtake each other. This was, after all, a country home that she'd created for herself, now wasn't it?

She wondered, more and more, if there *were* deer living in those woods.

*

Another year passed. Sometimes, thin white clouds would move across the blueness past her window. There were almost always birds, sometimes whole flocks of them. They never came too close, but she could make out the shapes of doves and thrushes, even the occasional hawk. Their presence delighted her.

The church bell started to ring on Sunday mornings. Very softly at first. But then, loudly enough to sometimes wake her up. And she always smiled when her eyes came open. She had never been much of a religious person, but Grace sometimes thought of going to that church.

The best of all, though? She'd occasionally spot dark shapes emerging from the trees, when she went into her bedroom. Spindly shapes, moving very timorously. Only for an instant. They would seem to sense her gaze on them, and retreat in a flash.

If she was very patient – Grace kept on telling herself – then in time they might get more used to her. Even venture closer.

One night around the middle of June, though, there was a violent thunderstorm. The woodlands and the brook were lit up with continual violent flashes. And a bolt of lightning actually hit the steeple of the church. It was still smouldering come morning. Was that an ill omen? Nothing bad had ever happened to her pastoral retreat.

Grace started to feel uneasy again for the first time in a very long while. Could sense an awful heaviness to the air around her, as though something momentous were on its way.

It was Friday afternoon when she heard the sound of a vehicle approaching. She was totally nonplussed at first, having almost forgotten that noise.

When she looked up from her desk, though, she could see a small square black dot coming nearer. It resolved itself into the shape of a Grand Cherokee Jeep. It was ploughing straight across the open grasslands, leaving twin ruts in the sward. And was weaving quite badly, as though the person driving it was drunk.

Grace believed that it would come right up to her, at first. But then it suddenly veered away abruptly. Heading off, instead, towards the woodlands.

She had to go through to her bedroom, to observe the rest.

The big four-wheeler pulled up by the treeline. Both of its front doors swung open. Two dark figures stumbled out, and disappeared into the woods.

They were each holding something.

Within a few minutes more, she started hearing rifle-shots. Grace's hands went to her mouth. She quivered for her deer. But she felt entirely helpless, wholly frozen to the spot.

The shooting went on until darkness almost fell. And was followed by an awful, lengthy silence. Then, the motor started up again. Headlamps came on as the Jeep began to move.

Its progress was even less in a straight line than it had been before. Had the lengthy pause been filled up with more drinking?

A harsh beam of light came right in through her window, pinning her at first. But then she jumped out of the way of it. Was trembling. Had they seen her?

The headlamps grew, filling up the glass. And then they tipped off at an angle. The Jeep's motor stilled again – somewhere quite nearby, but out of sight.

Heavy-booted, staggering footsteps started to approach. And, mere moments after that, her front door was thumped on, gave its first of many shudders.

Grace began to scream for help.

But the sad fact was ... she was alone, in the middle of the countryside.

And no one came.

*

Jenny Tarlane, nineteen, fresh in from Wisconsin, went up to view the little apartment with her boyfriend Tad.

"The previous occupant," the landlord, Mr. Michov, told her, "made a good number of alterations."

Jenny was agog and breathlessly excited to be finally in New York.

She forgot about such things, however, when she got a look at what the 'previous occupant' had done.

"Oh my God, what was she *thinking*? I'll just have to strip the whole place out!"

Which was why, Michov pointed out, the rent was so reasonable.

She moved in the next day, and started mapping out her plans. That awful panelling would have to go, of course. That grungy furniture. Those rugs.

But the first thing Jenny started on was scraping at the pictures glued so rigidly to both the windows.

What was the good of a city apartment, after all, without a city view?

*

Meg Torrance had lived alone all her life, in a house in the depths of Maine. Had always dreamed of living in New York, but she had never found the courage. Years ago, though, she'd stuck pictures of the city onto all of her numerous windows, so that she could at least have a view of the place.

Crowds bustled through them, these days. Yellow cabs went by. She didn't even think of them as simply 'pictures' any more.

And yet one view, from her second bedroom, interested her particularly today. Paper that had been there for a good couple of years, by now, was being scraped away from one small window in a grey apartment block.

After a while, she could see the face of a smiling young woman, peering out.

A police siren went by, outside her house, making her shudder. Meg never went out of doors these days, for fear of being mugged, or worse.

There were often days when she barely felt safe in her own home.

Beautiful Stranger

It wasn't long before I found myself just watching her for hours. Usually when she was sat in front of the TV, which was something she always did with all the lights off.

She would sit there in the darkness of my living room, the cathode rays making her so-very-pale skin glow as luminously as some dashboard Virgin Mary's. Sitting ramrod straight, despite the fact that she was in an easy chair. Her delicate, cool hands folded neatly in her lap. Her pale blue eyes hardly blinking at all.

The expression on her face? It never altered, whatever she might be watching. A sit-com. A science documentary. An action movie, or a news broadcast on starvation in Africa. It never got the smallest of responses from the tiniest of the muscles in her face.

There was nothing at all haughty about the way that Cheryl looked. About the way that *any* of the Risers looked. Nothing supercilious or aloof.

Just ... detached.

Perhaps 'disconnected' would be the slightly better word.

And – after a long while of this – she would realise that she was being watched. Her face would turn towards me. Her incredible, ethereally-beautiful face, like the visage of an angel.

She would take in the fact that I was there, and submerged in observing her. She'd blink.

But her expression did not alter. Not a touch.

Those first few weeks, the idea grew up in my head that she really was smiling, but inside.

*

I'd first seen a living human being actually out with a Riser about a year back.

'Out'? As in 'stepping out'.

As in dating.

It had been at a bar on the far fringe of Soho, fashionable enough to attract clientele like us, but not so trendy as to be packed full to bursting. I'd been there with my then girlfriend, Lois, her younger sister and her sister's handsome boyfriend, and another couple that I knew through work. That last pair? They would realise the dynamics of this particular evening after another hour or so. Look at each other, and silently admit that they had no wish to join in. Turn uncomfortably quiet on us, make their excuses a while later, and depart. Leaving us last four to finish up our drinks and head back to my pad nearby, where we could get more intimate.

Lois's sister was gorgeous, even prettier than her. I was already looking forward to it. But – this early in the evening – it was simply trendy cocktails at a marginally trendy bar. Just that, on the surface.

Till the door swung open, and the middle-aged woman stepped in with a tall Riser on her arm. You can spot them immediately, thanks to their utter paleness and the noticeable way they move.

"Oh my *God*, Geoff !" Lois immediately whispered, in the kind of *sotto voce* you can hear across an entire room.

The woman didn't bat an eyelid, however, although she must have heard it. She was obviously quite used to reactions of that kind.

We'd all read about this phenomenon, of course, the living hooking up with the walking, risen dead. Just last month, for instance, Cosmo had run a piece entitled *Cool Boyfriend: The Pros and Cons of Dating Risers*. But we'd never actually seen it until now.

The couple chose a small table about a dozen feet across from us. One of the bar staff came over to them, rather stiffly, and the woman ordered wine and food.

Then gazed back at her companion almost rapturously.

She was one of those women in her mid-forties who seemed to have aged badly through circumstance rather than self-neglect. Too much of a stoop to the shoulders. Too many lines etched into what had once been an attractive face. A permanent down-turn to the corners of her mouth, and a watery sadness to the eyes that could never be blotted away.

Decades of disappointment, then, written into her leathery features. Faithless husbands? Careless children? Younger boyfriends who had used her and then left? You can never know what people's histories are unless they, or someone, tells. But you can take an even guess.

And her companion ... must have been in his late twenties when he'd died. He was slightly over six foot tall, with the build of a rugby-player. Short-cut, curly, sandy-coloured hair. Emerald green eyes. Dressed like something out of a good catalogue – had she dressed him, or was that his natural instinct?

And how good-looking?

I'll get to that subject later.

Anyway, the wine turned up. He poured, with utter smoothness and precision. She raised her glass towards his, and they clinked.

Her gaze hadn't left his face, almost the whole while they'd been in here. And what exactly was she seeing there? I wondered at the time.

Lois screwed her features up. Her sister ducked her head and made that finger-down-throat gesture.

I just watched.

When the food turned up, the Riser took a little of his own on his fork, held it out towards the woman to taste. Again, had she trained him to do that, or did he do it naturally?

But I can still remember her expression, to this very day. She looked as though brilliant sunlight had just rushed straight through her body. As though she had momentarily been brushed by the wing of an angel.

After another while, the six of us forgot about them, or rather managed to ignore them. Got back to the business in hand that evening.

But I can *still* remember the expression on that woman's face.

I can remember something else as well, now that I think about it. Shame I didn't think about it sooner.

The way that she stared deep into the Riser's eyes. It was not simply adoration. It was more as though ... she were trying, very hard, to find something in there.

And, when I look at Cheryl's face these days, is my own gaze the same?

*

It is generally accepted these days that the presence of the risen dead in all developed countries has been caused by the widespread use of Revenox. I can't give you its clinical name, since it stretches several paragraphs. But never has the commercial name for any drug turned out to be quite so prophetic.

A wonder-drug in its day, though its use is now banned worldwide. It accelerated the healing of traumas, in some cases sixfold. Was used for injuries, to flesh and bones and even nerve tissue. For recovery after any kind of surgery. Even for dental work.

It couldn't heal the damage of a heart attack, or repair the brain after a stroke. But if something, anything, had put a hole or a break in your body, Revenox could close it up in more than record time.

And it always *did* work the best on the young and fit, those who healed the fastest anyway.

The 'side-effect' only became apparent several more years down the line.

The first is always the most famous one. Sven Ollson, a young ad exec from Stockholm rather too fond of the cocktail of strong vodka and fast cars. Went into a lamppost one night, punching the engine block right back into the driver's seat. Which was no real problem, because Sven hadn't put his seatbelt on, and had already sailed out head-first through the windshield. Dead before he hit the ground, his neck snapped.

One hour on, his wounds start healing, the damage repairing itself.

Three hours on, the gashes are all closed up, leaving not even a faint pink mark.

Before dawn, he's on his feet and moving round.

This kind of charming thing kept happening more and more. The scientists are still trying to figure it out, but realise now that Revenox caused changes on a very deep, genetic level.

And at first? Our governments locked all these quiet, pale folk up, to study them. Until the Civil Rights groups got in on the act.

Final judgement? The Risers were still human, and they had done nothing wrong. At least, it seemed rather curmudgeonly by that point to arrest poor Sven for drunk driving.

There are plenty of them by now. Mostly men, but a reasonable percentage of women.

You see, those who die of old age, or from heart attacks or strokes or cancer, simply do not rise. It is those who've had an accident or somesuch. Motorbikes, or driving too fast. Contact or dangerous sports. Fistfights. Going out with a bunch of friends one evening, getting blasted, stepping out into the traffic.

Which means, consequently, that the vast majority of Risers are the young and fit. Quite a few of them, in fact, used to be criminal gang members, killed in turf wars.

And as for their looks? I told you that I'd get to that.

Well, let's just say that death becomes a lot of them. That very evident, almost translucent paleness to their skin. That inner stillness they possess, as though the galaxy revolves around them, they are its fixed core. The smoothness, the refined grace, of their every motion. The fixedness of their expressions, the steadiness of their gaze.

Forget shambling monsters, dragging themselves around, moaning, with flesh dropping off their bones. The zee-word has been binned alongside all those n's and c's, these days. They don't crumble come sunrise, and they don't eat living flesh.

A lot of the risen dead, in fact, are enviably beautiful.

*

Kath followed Lois. And Kelly followed Kath. Then there were Jane, Marsha, and Zoe.

It mostly wasn't me who broke it off. I enjoyed being with each of them. I have a way with women, you see, but to tell the truth it is limited. It has an expiry date. I can have them eating out of the palm of my hand for a short while. Get them to do anything I want. Lois's sister was my idea, for instance.

But after a few months, even weeks with me, women seem to give me a second, much harder look. And not particularly like what they see.

It's always bothered me, but not too much. I'm always ready to move on and, working in PR as I do, there's perpetually a fresh horizon to move on to.

I was now with ... let me see ... another Kelly. Kelly Two. Except I wasn't as of this warm evening. Kelly Too Strong-Willed By Far. I'd come home to find a note, and both her bags and all her clothing gone. She'd thought that she could change me, the note said, the handwriting more jagged than was usual.

But nothing at all had changed. I was only back to where I always was. My apartment now had that familiar dull echo.

I didn't fancy the idea of cooking supper, eating it, alone. So I went to the small pub at the corner of my quiet mews in Fitzrovia. It was dimly-lit. There were only two old men in there – it being a Monday night – and the bar was being tended by a straggly-haired Australian kid I'd never seen before. I ordered venison sausages, with mash and onion gravy, and a pint of cider to wash it down with. Was half way through the meal when the tall, strawberry-blonde Riser walked in.

I was struck immediately by her looks, exceptional even for her kind. She was about my height in her heels, slim without being too slim. Shapely. With small hands and feet. Tiny nose and ears. Her hair fell in one smooth sweep across her right shoulder to the small of her back.

And her eyes? It was hard to tell in this light, but they seemed the clearest of pale blues.

The Australian kid immediately looked uncomfortable. The two old codgers at the far end looked up, frowned disgustedly, then went back to conversing.

All the woman did was sit down at a corner table and...

And that. Nothing more. She just stared evenly into thin air.

It's unusual to see a Riser out completely on its own. Which doesn't mean they're all out on hot dates, Cosmo or not. Since they do not speak, and most people feel uncomfortable around them, they don't hold down jobs. Their families, their loved ones, even their close friends wind up having to look after them. And those who have none? There are state-run hostels for their kind these days, since we cannot have the risen dead just littering the streets (a shame we don't feel the same about the living, homeless charities point out).

Anyway, you rarely get a Riser wandering unaccompanied into a bar. Somebody would normally come with them just to make sure they got served, if nothing else.

It was turning out to be a less than normal night.

So, after some five minutes of this, the kid behind the bar plucked up the nerve to come across to her and mutter quickly, "Drink?"

She looked up at him, nodded, then stared into space again.

He hadn't had the sense to ask her what kind. Just poured her a half of lager, put it down in front of her, and went away again.

The woman picked up the glass, took a tiny sip. The bridge of her nose screwed up the next instant. She put it back down and just seemed to forget about it.

I must have watched her for the best part of the next half hour. Taking in, not just her beauty. Taking in her utter stillness. She was like ... not a photograph, nor even a painting really. Like a figure etched in stained glass, in the high window of some cathedral. Had an ethereal, quite unworldly quality I'd never seen before.

And I realised something about myself, during that half hour of watching. Ever since that first evening, that middle-aged woman in that marginally-smart bar, these Risers had ... fascinated me, somehow. To the very core.

Why so deeply? I am still not sure, even now. Maybe they simply possess something that I've always craved. A total inner calm, perhaps. Or absolute detachment.

Whatever. In the end I couldn't help myself. I had to get up closer, try to find out more about one.

This one in particular.

Faltering only slightly, I picked up the dregs of my drink, and walked over to her table.

Had to clear my throat before I was able to speak.

She looked up at me and, yes, her eyes proved to be an extremely pale blue.

"Is it alright if I join you?" I asked.

She gave me another tiny nod, her gaze fixed on my face now. It stayed there when I sat down.

I could almost feel the kid at the bar staring at my back by this time. Thinking that I was some kind of pervert? I didn't much care.

"Lager doesn't seem to be your drink," I pointed out to her. "Would you like something else?"

She nodded.

"Wine?"

She didn't respond.

"Er, a cocktail? A martini? G&T?"

This was already becoming a preposterous encounter, I realised. What exactly was I going to do? Run through the entire list of beverages, from A to Z, until she gave another nod. I stopped.

And it was then I noticed something gleaming at her throat. Something gold. A little pendant, with a name picked out on it in curlicues.

Cheryl.

I said it out loud.

"That's your name then?"

And she nodded.

She had to be twenty-three or -four. Quite stunning.

"Aren't you with anyone, Cheryl? A boyfriend? A husband? Parents? There has to be *someone* looking after you."

She was very clean and neatly dressed, in mid-price-range designer clothing, so that last had to be true enough. But she didn't respond to any of my questions. Whoever she had been with, had she simply walked away from, left?

"Do you live nearby, perhaps? Can I take you anywhere?"

No reaction whatsoever. All she did was stare into my face intensely.

I thought of asking her if she wanted anything to eat. Until I realised that would present the same problem as the drink had.

My mind was becoming, simultaneously, stuttery and numb. At a loss as to which direction to go next. What next to do? What next to say?

There was nothing I could think of. This had not been such a good idea at all.

So, "Okay then," I told her. "I'll just leave you be. I'm sorry to have disturbed you."

Then I got up quickly, headed for the door.

It was only when I stopped by the kerb, to take a few deep breaths, that I realised she had followed me outside.

*

Fascinated all over again, I let her follow me the whole way home. She moved when I moved, at the same pace. And she stopped when I stopped. How far would this go? I was wondering now. How far exactly could I take this?

Maybe that has always been my attitude to attractive women. Maybe that has always been the problem.

I was already starting to think about her the same way I thought about the Loises and Kelly's and the Marsha's, only more beautiful, quieter. Not as risen dead at all.

Even so, I could scarcely believe it when I pushed open the front door of my flat and she walked in behind me. I wasn't afraid. Risers had been around for years, there was not one recorded instance of them harming anyone.

I went through into the living room, switched on the lights.

Only for her to switch them *off* again a moment later. That made me jump, I must confess.

But she didn't advance on me, her slavering jaws agape. She simply crossed the room to my favourite chair, sat down in it – bolt upright. And then picked up the remote and switched the TV on.

Its light washed across her so-pale skin, making it seem to glow.

That was the start of it.

*

She watched the screen till midnight, not changing the channel nor reacting in any way to what was on there. Her gaze didn't even falter when adverts came on.

But finally, she simply clicked the thing off. On what signal? Stood up in the dark, then wandered down my hallway till she found the bedroom.

I was following *her* by now, like some zoologist studying a mammal.

She simply ... went inside, turned back my duvet. Stripped down to her underwear, revealing a body that was as flawlessly lovely as her face. Climbed into my bed and fell immediately asleep, with the light still on.

And that seemed to be that.

Except I sat down in the bedroom's single chair, and watched her for several more hours before I finally dozed off.

*

She was not there, come morning. Just an impression where she'd lain. She was in the kitchen, making breakfast. Only for herself.

Black coffee. A bowl of muesli. I watched her start on it, then remembered that I ought to eat myself.

I tried talking to her again a few times, but I got no reaction. In the end, I simply had to go to work.

She'll be gone by the time I return home, I kept telling myself. *She'll simply wander off again.*

Was there any regret, bound up with that thought? I just wasn't sure.

But I opened my front door that evening to the noise and flicker of the television set, emanating from a darkened living room once more. She was in the same position she had been last night, watching a report about a bomb in Tel Aviv. Then she watched a game show. Her expression did not change.

I made no attempt to talk with her, this time. Simply went about my normal business, working around her as though she were some great big block of marble that had somehow wound up in my living room. Cooked and ate my supper. Loaded the dishwasher – a job overdue. Wrote out a few cheques for bills in the glow from the kitchen door.

Kept on looking at her, studying her, though.

What had fascinated me about her kind before – and what struck me so forcibly about her now, I realised – was that they all seemed so entirely...

There was only one word for it.

Perfect.

Human beings? They're never that. There's always a blemish, a tic, a flaw just waiting to be found.

But perhaps, it was beginning to occur to me, I was playing in a different league now.

"Cheryl?"

I said it from the doorway when she went through to my bedroom once again.

She stopped, in her lacy underwear. Turned, and gazed at me.

"What exactly are you doing? Do you realise this is my home? How long are you planning to stay? Are you planning to move in for good?"

Gazed at me. That was all she did. The sole response I got.

I should have been unnerved, but was not. I was still too fascinated by her.

Once again, she fell asleep with the light on.

She hadn't pulled the duvet over her this time, though. I studied her body. The semi-liquid flow of the limbs, and the smooth sweep of the curves. The loveliest female body I had ever seen – and I'd seen more than a few.

After a long while, something new began occurring to me. I had spoken to her, but I'd never touched her. Never touched any Riser.

And what did it feel like?

Cool, I knew that. Risers aren't stone-cold, of course. How could they *possibly* be that? They would be room temperature at the very least. But the truth is that they run at about five degrees below a living human, and so feel cool to our touch.

Otherwise?

Stiff? Or clammy? If she was either of those, I'd throw her out and burn the sheets. No, correct that – burn the bed!

But slowly, I went over to her, taking care my shadow didn't fall across her face. Stood for an age near the corner of the mattress, trying to convince myself I didn't need to do this.

Finally, I just reached down and brushed my fingertips across her wrist.

Drew them back quickly enough ... that coolness *was* unsettling.

But it was nothing like I had supposed. Nothing like dead meat, the chill of perished flesh.

Rather, it seemed to be a part of what she was. It suited her.

When I touched her for a second time, my palm stayed gently on her forearm.

Her eyes suddenly slid open. Those very pale blue eyes. And I jerked back, embarrassed and rather frightened.

She just gazed into my face. There was no accusation in her stare. No discomfort or displeasure.

In fact, precisely nothing. Her expression was the same as when she watched bomb-mangled bodies. The same as when she watched quiz shows.

My voice was hoarse when I finally asked her, "Did you mind me doing that?"

But she simply went to sleep again.

*

Over the course of the next couple of weeks, I took in certain facts. That she seemed to have moved in for the duration. And – that being the case – there were new tasks assigned to me. Extra food was no problem, I took notice of what she seemed to like and what she didn't, shopped accordingly. But she couldn't wear the same clothes forever. Or the same underwear for that matter.

I spent some evenings after work on Bond Street and in Burlington Arcade, buying a new wardrobe for her.

Found myself hoping that she would smile at what I'd purchased. Or, at the very least, her eyes would sparkle.

They never did, though she wore the clothes. She didn't even mind me watching her while she changed into them. Even the underwear.

She'd give me a twirl sometimes, once she was all dressed up. But no, she never smiled.

Two whole weeks. We didn't go out. And – despite breaking up with Kelly Two – I didn't see anyone else.

Perhaps, it started to occur to me, because I was *already* seeing someone.

We never clashed. She never disagreed with me, even silently. I had never been with a companion like that.

If I wanted to watch a specific show, for instance, and she had a different channel on, I'd simply reach across and change it. She'd continue watching without so much as a puzzled blink.

Most of the time, though, I wound up looking straight at her, instead of the programme I'd switched over to, becoming enthralled by her utter, perfect beauty. Cheryl was enchanting me.

Who had she been? What had she once done? Where had she come from? There were no possible answers to these questions, and I turned them over less and less as the days passed. Realising that they were not important, since I simply didn't care.

She was one of the risen dead. But did that matter? I kept on asking myself. Maybe she was what I'd never found in any normal woman.

Enchanted, did I say? Entranced.

In which case, why didn't I go outdoors with her? Introduce her to my friends?

I had to admit it to myself in the end, the cynic in me winning over. She'd become my dirty little secret.

Just how dirty, though?

I couldn't make that mental leap as yet. But I had taken to buying clothes and underwear for her she simply didn't need. Very sexy clothes and underwear, just to watch her try them on then wear them round the flat. Though I didn't even need to go to that expense to see her get undressed.

She bathed and showered regularly. The expression on her face if I walked into the bathroom while she was in there?

The same expression as she ever wore. A total lack of pleasure or surprise, certainly. But a lack of disapproval too. And women always wound up giving me a look of disapproval.

Two weeks turned into three, and the harder questions kept on gnawing at me like a pack of rats. Had we now become a couple? Or had she simply become my plaything, my pale, life-size dress-up doll?

I couldn't decide which. But knew I'd have to.

*

It was a Saturday night by this time, the West End erupting around my quiet mews like a firework display with shouting people, blaring music, motor horns and drunks instead of rockets.

Cheryl and I sat in my darkened living room, the wash of the TV screen playing across us both.

She had showered just recently. One towel was wrapped around her body, and the other formed a turban in her hair. Again, I was gazing at her, trying to remember when I had ever seen anything as lovely.

And ... if I could only really please her. Make her, for once, smile. *Was* she smiling, inside?

A little of the night's noise drifted in through my partially-open window, despite my flat's secluded location. And maybe it was that which made something occur to me.

Going Back

Why not go right back to the beginning, when we'd met? Since I believed I had the answer now?

"Cheryl?" I asked.

Her face turned towards me, only one half of it lit-up in the cathode glow.

"*Would* you like a drink?"

My heart was thumping when she nodded.

"Champagne?"

Why hadn't I thought of it that first night? I've yet to meet any woman who doesn't like champagne.

She gave me a second nod. Though not a smile.

I went and got a bottle from the fridge, two glasses. Poured it for us. Almost clinked the glasses, until I remembered that middle-aged woman in the bar.

She sipped it. Didn't show me any pleasure, though her nose did not screw up either.

But, half way through my second glass, I sat right up close to her, on the edge of what had now become *her* chair. And started telling her exactly how I'd come to feel.

How utterly perfect she was. How beautiful, how calm and very gentle. And how comfortable – serene even – I felt in her presence. I had never been with anyone like her. We were right for each other, whatever the rest of the world might think.

And her expression as I said this?

Suicide-bomb victims and quiz shows. Being watched naked. Or eating muesli.

That didn't stop me. It had all been building up for weeks now, nothing would. The last of my inhibitions? Stripped away by the champagne.

She *was not* dead, I kept telling myself. Dead meant lying in the ground. And she was not that thing.

I buried my face into hers. Her cool lips. Her cool cheek. Her lashes batted, once, against my own. There was nothing unsettling about her temperature now. It soothed me and relaxed me.

And then, I was lifting her tenderly out of the chair. Laying her on the floor.

Distant laughter filtered through my window.

Then I was on top of her, and then inside her coolness.

It was over very quickly. Far too quickly – I'd been waiting too long. I moaned, pressed my face into the smooth, pale flesh above her shoulder.

Finally, lifted my head.

Stared down for a moment, at her face lit by the TV's glow.

Then rolled off her, curled myself into the tightest ball I could. And remained in that position for almost the entire night.

Because ... that middle-aged woman in that passably-trendy bar, the way that she had stared into her handsome Riser's eyes?

I had at last come to realise what she had been looking for.

*

That was all nine months ago. Cheryl is still here, and still exactly as she first was.

Myself? I wish I could say the same. I've lost about twelve pounds, so that my clothes hang off me. A gaunt, skeletal, red-eyed stranger peers back at me from the mirror, when I bother with it at all, which is rare. I don't worry too much about my appearance these days. It's not like I'm out there searching for a date or anything.

My firm has noticed though, and my boss is thinking of dropping me.

Maybe I'd better smarten up. I need that job, after all, to keep on looking after Cheryl properly.

I feed her, trying out new dishes on her, hoping one will please. I clothe her and I even bathe her.

And I make love to her every night. Not like that first time, but for hours, as slowly and considerately as a man can manage.

Because I'm *still* looking for it, you see. The same thing that prematurely-aged woman was trying to capture.

Not even a smile. I don't even need that. Not even a sparkle in the eyes.

Just ... the tiniest gasp. The tiniest flutter. A momentary squeeze-shut of the eyelids, or even a slight change in the rhythm of her breath.

Something, *anything*, which shows that she's responded to me.

Something, *anything*, which proves she really *is* smiling inside.

Going Back

I know that she's attracted to me. I know she has to like me, even care about me in her way. Why would she have followed me home in the first place otherwise? Why would she have stayed? I only have to find the proper way to draw that feeling out.

And you think I'm cracked? You think that I have an alternative? What, go back to the Loises and Kellys, after this?

No, I can't do that.

Occasionally – in a particularly reflective moment – I might think about B-movie zombies, eating human flesh.

But, as I have shown all along, the risen dead are not that ... they are graceful, even delicate beings.

And perhaps have found more delicate, more subtle methods of devouring and destroying humans like myself.

What Malcolm Did The Day Before Tomorrow

Almost all mistakes are ones of timing.

So, if Malcolm Cowper hadn't overslept by half an hour, if he hadn't missed his Amsterdam Canal Cruise and had to hang around another forty minutes until the next barge arrived, if he hadn't ordered a second beer to wash down his massive Dutch savoury pancake at lunch, if he hadn't been so moved by the Anne Frank house that he'd back-tracked through the echoing rooms to see it all over again, if he hadn't been so awed by the tall pale redhead at her window in the Red Light District that he had contrived to walk past three times – then he'd have never wound up at the counter of the Krimson Devil coffeeshop at the same time as Silas Farrell.

It was October in the city, a late autumn taking the edge off the summer's heat. The sky's blue was a murky one now, phasing towards grey and there was, just sometimes, the faintest hint of drizzle on the air. You couldn't even see it, only feel its touch against your cheek.

Brown leaves clogged the narrow gutters, or floated on the dark canals like old, discarded memories. Evening was on its way. And Malcolm had already promised himself a special little treat.

If you want coffee in Amsterdam, you go to a café. The famous 'coffeeshops' – and there are hundreds of them – sell legalised dope.

It wasn't that he was a regular smoker. At parties maybe. Or after dinner, at the homes of certain types of friends. But the last time he'd been here in Amsterdam, a decade back, he had been seventeen. And he had been here with a whole big group of friends. And they had visited the coffeeshops every single evening, emerging staggering and laughing.

And that was what this trip was all about, wasn't it? Putting grown-up matters to one side for several days. Taking a break from his dull job back home.

A 'stickie', he remembered. *That was what they called a ready rolled-up joint round here.*

Malcolm went up to the counter, the thick smell of the shop's interior already making his head buzz, and asked the young man who was leaning on the far side of it, "A blond hash stickie, please?"

Which was when the figure standing next to him snorted and then murmured something.

Malcolm looked around. Found himself gazing into a round, long-nosed and very smooth face, sporting an Imperial beard, a huge walrus moustache, and very flinty eyes. They all belonged to a short hippie in sandals and embroidered denims, with his hair down to his jeans' belt

"Excuse me?" Malcolm said to him, in English. Everybody here spoke English. "Did you just say something?"

"Kid's stuff," the man repeated in a strong American accent.

Malcolm's 'stickie' turned up on a saucer, and the hippie's eyes went down towards the thing. "Blond hash? That's for teeny-boppers."

"All a question of taste," Malcolm answered.

The man studied him from under hooded eyelids. "You a Brit?"

"Yes I am, in fact."

"I love you guys. You crack me up. Like that dude on 'Buffy', you know – ? 'Good gracious, I actually do believe the universe is going to be destroyed by Upchuck Demons in – well, gosh – the next five minutes!'"

Malcolm felt a hint of unease. There was something about this character which was definitely off-putting. He looked ... twenty three, twenty four at the most? But the way he spoke, the way he acted. It set off alarm bells. He could only think of two ways someone of this age could have become hard-bitten. Criminality. Hard drugs.

Either way, he wanted nothing of it.

So he said, "That's remarkable. What an astonishing impersonation. You have a real talent there and I think that, if you really tried, you could make a bloody good living from it. And now, if you'll kindly let me be ...?"

And with that, he took himself and his stickie off to a table in the farthest corner of the room.

When he glanced back towards the counter again, the little man was facing away, only his long hair visible. Thank God.

It was dim in here, the tables lit up by small candles in stained red glass jars. There were posters on the walls that went back twenty, thirty years. Most of the other clientele were men, and there was a dreamy casualness about the place that he had been craving for months now.

There was a matchbook on the table, with a hysterically laughing little red devil printed on it. Malcolm opened it and lit the joint.

Inhaled. Held it. Then breathed out in a long stream. Leaned back. A broad smile went through his whole body.

By the time he'd finished half the spliff, there were no hard edges left to the shape of his wandering thoughts.

The hippie sat down opposite him, staring at him intently. Oh no! Malcolm almost burst out laughing.

"You again?"

"Yeah. But look here, I'm so sorry, man. I get the feeling that I might have, like, offended you somehow."

"Oh no, not at all."

The American offered his hand. "Silas Farrell, by the way. Of Newark, New Jersey, originally."

Who the hell got called 'Silas' these days? "Er, Malcolm Cowper. Of East Finchley, London."

"Pleased ta meecha, Malcolm. And look, if you want me to just go away, I'll do it. But I'd hate to think I caused offence to a nice-seeming guy like yourself. And if there's any way that I can – ?"

"I *told* you," Malcolm broke across him. "I was not offended."

"Not even a little bit. Can you look me squarely in the eye and tell me that I caused you not the tiniest discomfort? So I'm gonna make it up to you the best way I know how. Stub out that pathetic hash joint, brother. I'm gonna introduce you to some of the real stuff."

And he produced a little plastic bag out of one denim pocket.

"That's not opium, is it?" Malcolm asked amusedly. "'Cause I don't do any hard stuff – you *do* understand that?"

"No, bro, this is just a simple smoke. But a hundred times better than that bullshit. It comes from the Dutch East Indies."

He was rolling a spliff all the while he spoke, tearing off the printed cover of the matchbook to use as a roach. A joint with a little devil in it. Malcolm felt intrigued.

"First time here in Amsterdam?" Farrell asked him, conversationally.

And if Malcolm hadn't already been stoned, then perhaps he wouldn't have gone on to explain the reason for his visit. By the end of it, Silas Farrell was grinning broadly.

"That's just perfect, then. Your first full day back here in this wonderful city of ours. A free and single man, reliving the wild days of his youth. That's *beautiful*, my friend!"

He screwed up the tip of the finished joint tightly, and lit it.

Offered it to Malcolm.

Who took it between two tentative fingers. Studied it for a moment. Raised it to his lips.

"Hold it a moment," Silas Farrell said.

Malcolm peered at him, almost annoyed. Was this a joke?

"Just before you try the stuff, here's something you should do. Hold an image in your mind. Something that really pleases you. The best thing that you've seen all day here. Can you do that, friend?"

Yes, of course he could. Except ... the best thing that he'd seen all day? Malcolm had packed so many good sights into the last few hours. He turned the options over.

And then realised.

Malcolm put the paper to his mouth. Inhaled.

He closed his eyes.

*

The realisation that he was now moving opened them again. He was on his feet and walking, in the open air. No longer in the coffeeshop which – he realised when he looked around – was not even in sight.

He was actually back in the Red Light District. Evening was no longer coming, and several of the people passing by him seemed familiar.

He stopped, turned around. Was this a hallucination? He wasn't scared in the slightest, though. Felt entirely happy and relaxed.

He continued down the towpath, realising something new. There were prostitutes in many of the windows he was passing. And the vast majority of them didn't attract him in the slightest. But a few more windows down he knew that...

He came to a halt, in front of the tall redhead with her ice-cream skin he'd gawped at several times before.

And didn't walk on by, as he had done the last occasion.

He went in.

Her name turned out to be Krystal, though he doubted that was real. She slid shut the curtain on her window. They got to it.

He had always imagined this would be a passionless experience. Instead ...?

They did it on the bed. On the floor. On top of her washbasin, in her shower, against the wall. They did it him on top, her on top, side by side, doggie fashion, spooning. They sweated and heaved and tried to outdo each other in the sheer amount of noise that they could make.

Two hours later, he was tiredly pulling his clothes back on when something occurred to him.

"Er ... shouldn't I, er, pay you or something?"

Krystal, who was sprawled across a chaise longue by this time, gave him a luscious smile. "Forget it. It was just a pleasure."

Evening was approaching by the time that he emerged onto the street again. Malcolm stood there for a while, blinking rather dazedly and trying to figure out what had just happened. Was he imagining all of this?

He quickly worked out what the answer had to be. He had dozed off on Krystal's bed for a few minutes, a much-earned post-coital nap, and dreamed about the Krimson Devil coffeeshop and Silas Farrell.

He decided to test his theory out. Retraced the steps he thought that he had taken before, back to the bridge across the canal, then a right-hand turn towards the city centre.

And there, some eighty yards along, was the Krimson Devil coffeeshop, just as he had dreamt it.

At the counter, as he went inside, was a short, denim-clad, sandaled hippie, his back to the door.

Malcolm swallowed, started to approach. And the hippie turned towards him, grinned with recognition, and said:

"Hi there again, Malcolm. You look like you've had yourself a really groovy time."

*

"The strangest thing of all?" Silas Farrell told him. They were now back at the same table they had occupied the first time. "It ain't even magic, man. It's science. And to be precise, it's Albert friggin' Einstein."

Malcolm could only stare at the man, trying to take all this in.

"You heard of Relativity? Understand how it works? Well, you know how when you're bored time seems to pass by awful slow? Or when a lot of things are happening it seems to go extremely fast? What Einstein decided was – that's the way things really are. Time actually is relative.

"Now of course, that's not much use to us. We arrange to meet at eight, time's been passing fast for me and I turn up too early. So we have to have a constant to measure it all against – the speed of light, for instance. But it doesn't change the fact that, on one level, time *actually is relative*. Which means that it's affected by our perceptions of it. And our perceptions, surely, include memory and *deja vu*? What the dope does is fuse the two together far more tightly, tight as clams. Perception and reality."

"So I *did* imagine all of that?"

"No, you still don't get it." Farrell scratched his nose. "You actually did go back a couple of hours. The rest of the *world* didn't, don't get me wrong here. The rest of the *world* kept moving forwards at the same old pace. But your perception of time altered your personal experience of it."

His small eyes brightened when he saw that it was finally sinking in.

"So it's like ... I was in my own time-zone, as though inside a bubble?"

"Right."

"And I could move that bubble back against the normal flow of hours and minutes?"

Farrell gave a massive, cheesy grin. "Now that's what I *call* time-tripping! Huh?"

"So how did you come across this stuff?" Malcolm asked him now.

Farrell pursed his lips and then leant right back in his chair.

"When I first came here from the States, it was in the late Seventies."

Malcolm just gawped harder, because Farrell could barely have been *born* by the late Seventies.

"I made friends with this bunch of freaks, and they invited me come live with them in this big old squat on Van Rookjerinstraat. Anyhow, I was in the loft one day, and I came across this old chest full of nautical stuff and some really crumbly, leather-bound journals. All written in Dutch, of course.

"I got one of the local boys to translate them for me. And it turns out that the house used to belong to an olden time sea captain name of Pieter van der Hooge. And this van der Hooge, he's writing about this tiny little island he came across in the Dutch East Indies, with an aboriginal tribe on it. All of them young-looking, all of them very happy. And they put this down to this wild herb they smoke. I can't even pronounce the name, but it roughly translates as 'Angel which banishes the Demon of Tomorrow'. And right at the bottom of the chest, all wrapped up in oilskins, there's this enormous – like *enormous* – bale of the same stuff.

"Now, it has to be at least a hundred years old, and it's all dried up. And I'm thinking it can't be much use any more. But I try a little, and when I see how it works I just grab that bale and split, and I've been taking a few tokes every day for the last two-and-a-bit decades."

Farrell eased himself forwards again, allowing Malcolm to study his young and perfectly smooth features.

"I was born in 1955, Malcolm. And the way I look ain't down to Oil of Olay. I've been living the precise same day, any way I want to, since around the time you popped into existence. Sure, the rest of the world's moved on around me, I can see that. How else would I know about stuff like 'Buffy' otherwise? And how else would I get to meet you in the first place? But for me, I'm in this bubble, and tomorrow's never come. Eternal youth, man. True eternal youth, lived entirely in and for the moment."

Malcolm blinked at him so slowly he could almost hear his eyelids smack together. This little man was totally insane.

Except that didn't explain what he'd been through in the last couple of hours.

"But if I really *did* go back," he enquired carefully, "then why was the experience so terrific?"

"It's like any good dope, Malcolm," Farrell smiled. "It just makes you really happy."

He reached into his pocket and took out the plastic bag again, then dropped it on the table.

"Here, it's yours, enjoy. There's plenty more where that came from."

He even threw in a pack of skins.

*

His first impulse? To go straight back to Krystal. *But hold it*, Malcolm told himself. *Surely there are other things I can do with this stuff?*

He stopped in a doorway on an abandoned back-street, and then took the little bag out of his pocket and peered at its contents. Which certainly looked very old. A crumbly, coarse powder, dark brown, though there were a few small flecks of pale green and light ochre in it.

Malcolm started rolling himself a new joint.

What else of today had he enjoyed, besides the Red Light District? Well ... pretty much all of it, in fact. So why not start near the beginning?

He inhaled.

And was right on time for the canal cruise this time.

Just as he stepped onto the gangplank, the thin overcast above him suddenly dissolved, the sun broke through. The temperature of the air around him rose a couple of degrees. And so he re-did the canal cruise sprawled across a bench up near the prow with one arm dangling across the side. There was a fluted glass of champagne in his other hand, from which he sipped as they progressed. People waved to him from bridges. The light made the few remaining leaves on the towpath boughs translucent.

He went to the same bar for lunch. The savoury pancake was the most wonderful thing he'd ever tasted, and if nectar ever had a bitter tang to it, the beer was that.

He opted to give the Anne Frank house a miss afterwards and went to the Van Gogh Museum. It was not busy inside. Malcolm wandered round the ranked exhibits, losing himself in starry nights and springtime fields and the depthless yellow of giant sunflowers.

Three quarters of an hour in, he found himself talking with a flaxen-haired Canadian called Pamela. Half an hour later, they were having coffee at an outdoor table on the Leidseplein. And as evening started to approach, he found himself being led by the hand through the door of her hotel room.

I wonder, he thought, as she finally disappeared into the bathroom and the shower started running.

He rummaged through his clothes till he found the plastic bag, quickly rolled a joint and lit it.

And was being led by his hand through the door again.

Her lovemaking was even better than before.

The wonder of it was, he finished up no more tired than he'd been the first time. How on earth was that?

Malcolm realised the truth of the matter. He and Pamela had *not* made the beast with two backs twice in a row. His going back in time meant that they'd actually only done it once, albeit a revised and improved once. If he wanted to, he could go through it all again a dozen times in quick succession, without flagging in the slightest.

Anyway, twilight had fully enmeshed the city by this time. He chose a restaurant at random, ordered dinner. The food was wonderful. And, although he was seated on his own again by this time, he quickly got talking with the people at adjacent tables, who were interesting and bright.

"Where are you heading on to?" they all asked him.

They took him to the Melkweg, the long-established music venue round the corner on Lijnbaansgracht. There was a disco on this evening, the whole place packed to the rafters. Malcolm drank and danced, and shouted things to laughing, friendly strangers, and found punk girls and Goth girls and nouveau-hippy girls wrapping their arms around his neck and kissing him out of nowhere.

Then he went into the washroom, lit another joint, and did the whole thing over again.

*

He awoke in his hotel room feeling completely refreshed, but it was still dark outside. Malcolm glanced at the clock on the nightstand.

It showed 11:59. And that couldn't be right, since he was sure he'd been asleep for hours. Was it broken? Malcolm fumbled for his watch.

The luminous dials told him the same. He waited for them to move, for a good five minutes. Nothing.

That was bizarre. He sat up, puzzled.

It was perfectly quiet on the street outside. And the hotel was as silent as a graveyard. He had to have woken in the smallest hours of the night, when the whole city was dormant. He lay back again, trying to drift off. But couldn't. He became increasingly bored and restless.

The bag of dope – half worked into – and the little pack of skins were lying on his bedside cabinet beside the useless clock.

That struck him as odd, suddenly. Half of the stuff gone? Why? Every time he'd back-tracked today, his energy had been intact. And his pocket as full of cash as when he'd started out. But the weed itself was dwindling, obviously a non-renewable resource.

He couldn't figure it out exactly, but – apparently – the only thing the drug did not affect was its own self. It seemed immune to its own process.

Weird. But, after an interminable period of waiting, Malcolm thought, *why not?* One final time? Anything was better than this tedium.

So he sat up again, a sly grin creeping across his face. And proceeded to send himself backwards into Krystal's waiting arms.

*

This repeated evening – he had already decided – was absolutely, definitely his last. It was time to get back to his normal life. So when people started talking to him at the Japanese place just off Kerkstraat, he was polite to them, but made it clear he wished to be alone.

His watch was working fine by now, he realised as he raised his glass.

Once sated, he strolled towards Rembrandt Square. He could hear music and shouting up ahead, and was intrigued by the commotion.

It was coming from a little rock bar called *Matt Black*. There was a live band playing – he could not see the musicians because the place was so crowded. Malcolm pushed his way inwards till the stage came in sight. The five-piece group performing on it – two women and three young men – went under the name PVC. And they seemed to be a local group. Half the crowd were calling out their names, yelling encouragement.

They were just terrific. They played with skill and spirit and demented fervour, and the audience responded in kind. Ever since he'd arrived in this city, he had never known an atmosphere quite like this one.

Only one thing soured the experience slightly. Standing just ahead of him was one of the most beautiful blonde women he had ever seen, with a hundred-watt smile and a gracefulness to every movement he found wholly mesmerising. He'd have offered to buy her a drink straight away. The problem? The boyfriend she was hanging onto tightly. A good deal over six foot tall. Bald-shaven, in a leather waistcoat, with tattoos along his heavily-muscled arms.

So ... ought he?

He turned it over for a while, before finally giving in to the temptation. Then he snuck into the washroom and rolled yet another joint.

And was walking in through the front door again, pushing his way forwards through the crowd.

The band was even better than before, the audience crazier. And the blonde? She was no longer holding quite so tightly onto her huge boyfriend.

After a few moments, he appeared to tell her something that she really didn't like. She let go of him. An argument started between them, and seemed to grow more furious by the second.

The blonde shoved the big guy away from her. He responded by storming off.

For the next minute, she looked on the verge of tears. And when she started looking round her, there was bitterness in her perfect eyes.

Which alighted on Malcolm's face. She smiled tightly, and came over to him.

Her name was Maya, it turned out. She took him back immediately to her apartment nearby, climbed on top of him, and made love to him with harsh, silent ferocity.

By the time it was over, Malcolm was starting to feel rather guilty. She had done this out of spite and anger, not because she wanted him. And she'd been so happy with her boyfriend when he'd walked into *Matt Black*.

He got up from the bed slowly. The time was now 11:56.

He went through into the shower and spent a good ten minutes there, trying to let the water calm him down. What had he become, exactly? What was this drug turning him into? He would go back to his hotel room, and just put all of this behind him.

In the meantime...? Maybe he should tell Maya that, however her boyfriend had annoyed her, she'd be happier going back to him.

"You're very quiet?" he called into the bedroom.

There was no response. Had she fallen asleep?

He turned the shower off.

The bed, its sheets still crumpled, was entirely empty. Maya was nowhere in the room.

The alarm clock was now showing 11:59. Which couldn't possibly be right.

Malcolm stepped into the living room, and then the kitchen. Maya was not here in the apartment any longer. But this was her own home. What on earth would drive her out?

Despite the fact that it was only around midnight, it was very quiet indeed beyond the window. There was no one out there. Except ... it had been bustling when he had first arrived.

He dressed hurriedly and went out.

A lot of the cafés and restaurants still had their lights on, but were empty. Late-night shops had their doors wide open, yet were uniformly unattended. *What the hell?*

His head whirling slightly, Malcolm headed in the direction of Dam Square. Was this all some kind of joke?

The main square, like everywhere else, was utterly deserted.

An ornate clock gave the time as eleven fifty-nine, and refused to change its opinion on that, however long he stared at it.

An awful suspicion began to overtake him. Could this all be an effect of the drug that he'd been smoking?

The person to ask about such things was, obviously, Silas Farrell. So he headed back towards the Krimson Devil coffeeshop.

It was closed, a thick metal grille pulled down across the frontage. And so Malcolm couldn't see that he had any other choice.

He rolled another joint, inhaled it, closed his eyes.

When they re-opened, it was early evening again. The grille was up, the coffeeshop open. A short figure with hair down to its waist stood at the counter, as though waiting patiently.

Turned and grinned, when he walked in. Said, "Here we are all over again, Malcolm. I'll bet that you've been having yourself ..."

Then the smile and the voice both faltered.

"What's up?" Silas Farrell asked.

*

"Yeah, like, that's happened to me on more than a few occasions." They were back at the same table where they had first sat and spoken. "Either I doze off, or I'm having such a good time that I forget to backtrack, or whatever – and I hit the self-same barrier. 11:59."

He looked wholly relaxed about it. Which was more than Malcolm felt.

"I've thought it over quite a lot," Farrell informed him, "and the best rationale that I can come up with is, the whole thing's about perception, right? It's our *perception* that alters how time's working around us. And sure, we can perceive the present clearly enough, because it's right under our noses. We can perceive the recent past, because it's still fresh in our minds. But how clearly, by comparison, do we perceive the future?

"Consider it, brother. Really try to hold the future, even the near future, in your mind's eye. Tomorrow? Difficult, ain't it? Sure, you've got a vague idea of what it *might* be like. But it's an unknown quantity. And, compared to what happened to you half an hour back, it's about as clear as mud. Now, because that stuff I gave you works entirely by perception, it won't let you travel down a poorly-perceived route. So when you smoke this stuff, there's really no tomorrow to go into."

"Okay, okay, okay," Malcolm stammered, waggling his hands. "So let's say ... I stop smoking it completely, not another puff. How long would it take before it started to wear off?"

"I can't tell you exactly, since I've never tried to do it. But if it's like most other strong dope, I'd say you'd be coming down from it quite nicely – oh – some time around mid-morning tomorrow."

At which Malcolm sat bolt upright and yelped, "Mid-morning *when*? But you told me when you smoke this stuff, there's *no* tomorrow!"

Silas Farrell looked rather pensive for a moment, then said, "Well, like ... yeah. That's kinda the snag about this whole thing."

And he *still* seemed entirely at ease, unbothered. Until Malcolm pushed his chair back and stood slowly up, his face taut and his eyes blazing.

"Uh, Malcolm ...?"

Farrell clambered up himself, and started backing off.

"Hey, hey brother! What's the problem here?"

"You can't see that there's a *problem*? What the hell have you gone and done to me?"

"Whoa! Be reasonable a moment, dude."

Faces at the other tables started swinging round.

"I'm completely stuck here, aren't I? That's what you're telling me, 'bro'! I'm trapped in this one single day? And you're expecting me to be *reasonable* about it? Just what kind of monster are you?"

At which, Farrell stopped backing away and got angry himself. His face reddened, and then he exploded.

"Why you dull, dumb-assed suburban son-of-a-bitch! I'm a *monster*? I've done something *terrible* to you? And tell me, what exactly might that be? I've given you the greatest gift of all, if you could only see it! What precisely does tomorrow hold for you that's so terrific anyway? Going back to dumb East Finchley? Going back to your dumb job? Getting older, tired, disappointed? This way, you'll always be in your twenties! You'll live the same great day forever! And do you know – " he waved a trembling finger at the open door, "how many folks out there would give both arms to have what you've got? You ought to be down on your knees and *thanking* me, you idiot!"

It was that last bit, the 'thanking' bit, that finally made Malcolm snap. A strangled howl of rage emerged, and he just threw himself at Farrell, wrapping his fingers round the hippie's throat. They were both on the floor seconds later, Malcolm banging Farrell's hirsute skull repeatedly against it. He was going to *kill* him.

Probably would have, if the young man behind the counter hadn't vaulted over it and got him in a tight arm-lock.

Several of the other patrons helped to toss him out onto the sidewalk.

"We don't need that kind of unpleasantness in here, guy," one of them growled in his ear. "This is a peaceful place."

They stood blocking the entrance until he had gone away.

*

The drug had to wear off *some* time. All he had to do was wait.

Malcolm passed the evening in a daze. He walked until 11:45, and then made his way to Dam Square. There were plenty of people about. He waited under the same wall-clock, watched the baroque minute hand reach 11:59. It stopped there. Nothing changed at all around him, straight away. But after sixty more seconds – he counted them under his breath.

The square abruptly emptied. All the people, cars, and bicycles and trams in it just ... vanished, all in mid-acceleration or mid-loiter or mid-stride.

Everyone had gone into tomorrow. Everyone except himself and, somewhere, Farrell.

It was the most unnerving thing he'd ever seen. Malcolm had to fight hard not to panic once again. There were not even any pigeons left, he noticed. The hush began seeping through him like a deep, unnatural chill.

He had no practical way of measuring time, by now. His watch had stopped again. So he tried counting off the minutes in his head, but lost track by the first quarter of an hour. Sweet Jesus, how long was it going to take before things returned to normal?

It must have been a couple of hours – his instincts told him that – before he realised he was staying here to no good purpose. He still had his hotel room, his comfortable bed.

When he woke it was still dark, and his watch informed him that nothing had changed as yet.

Dam Square was the same yawning chasm when he re-approached it. He headed down Rokin, staring at the reflected lighting in the big canal.

Assuming he'd slept four or five hours, he had to have now used up at least a third of a day. And still nothing had changed about his circumstances. He stood it for what seemed a whole age longer, before admitting to himself that this was hopeless. Waiting passively just didn't seem to be the answer.

And he hated to admit the fact. But if there was any single person who might help him out of this predicament, it could only be Farrell. There *had* to be some kind of solution tucked away in that addled brain of his.

So Malcolm rolled another joint. Then went back to the coffeeshop.

*

There was no short figure here this time. Malcolm blinked uneasily, walked up to the counter and then peered at the young man behind it.

"Excuse me? Have you seen a hippie bloke in here, about so high, twenty three or four, waist-length hair, goes by the name of Silas Farrell?"

"You Malcolm Cowper?"

"Yes."

"He left a note for you."

Malcolm unfolded the thing and peered at it in the weak red light.

Malcolm, bro, it read. *I have an affection for you, genuinelly I do. But I cant abide vilence, specially when its directed against me. Ive decided to find myself another place to hang out from now on. Dont try to find me.*
Hopefully one day youll come to recognise the wonderfull gift that Ive bistowed on you. Till then –
Hang loose.
Silas Farrell.

The bloody hippie had run off, abandoning him to his fate. Well, they'd see about that, wouldn't they? He began to search for the man, painstakingly, street by street.

And quickly came to realise what a mammoth task that was. Amsterdam was brimming with all manner of hangouts. And that was just the centre. What if Farrell had chosen some distant suburb to lay low in?

Still, he had all the time he'd ever need to hunt the small man down. The dope, and its ability to take him backwards, made certain of that.

Except, he realised just before his fifth trip back...

That wasn't exactly the case. Not any longer.

He took the little bag out of his pocket once again. And suddenly noticed just how light it was. How easily it squished together in his palm.

Seven-eighths of the stuff was already gone.

When he thought through what would happen to him when the last of it ran out, he sat down on the spot and shuddered, his face in his hands, for a full half an hour. This just couldn't *be*.

Then he continued searching, moving at a jog. Hunted through every dark corner of every backstreet bar he came across. With no success whatever.

Several more times he tried waiting in Dam Square or his hotel room, pacing and dozing and still hoping to break through that moveless barrier, 11:59. With *still* no success whatever. It always ended the same way. He would be forced to roll another joint from his diminishing supply, and re-start the day over.

If only he could get more of the stuff. Maybe there was another bale hidden in the attic where Farrell had first found it? Where had that squat been he'd talked about? Van Rocco? Von Rookie?

Malcolm scoured a map until he found the right address. *Van Rookjerinstraat.* So he ran in its direction, actually skidding round the corner.

Only to be confronted by a double row of modern, red-brick town-houses, not an older structure anywhere in sight. They looked just a couple of years recent. The entire street had been demolished and rebuilt.

The only thing to do now was to redouble his efforts to find Farrell. Which was precisely what he did.

And did.

And kept on doing.

But – like some fat, lazy-looking bluebottle that is no longer there when your palm comes down on it – the man seemed to have vanished right off the face of the earth.

*

Malcolm woke and peered up. The same clock on the wall told him it was 11:59. He had fallen asleep on a statue's plinth.

Dam Square remained totally empty around him.

He took the bag out of his pocket, and studied its contents. All that remained was a little brown dust at the bottom. Malcolm swallowed hard.

But if there was any other choice at all, he couldn't see it.

He stood, rubbing gently at his limbs. And then went over to a doorway. Very carefully, he flattened out a paper on his knee. And then gingerly poured the remnants from the bag onto it.

Made sure that he got every last grain, and then rolled the whole thing tight. He squeezed it between his fingers, put it to his lips.

Thought of where he wanted to return this last time. He'd had a good while to consider that, and knew exactly.

Malcolm struck a match and raised it.

*

When he stepped in through Krystal's door, he told her immediately that he just wanted to talk, nothing else. And she smiled and said sure, that was fine.

She turned out to be – he'd never even bothered to find out before – a rather nice, intelligent person. Listened carefully as he told her all about Farrell and the strange, terrible dope. Even asked to see the latter.

All that he could show her was an empty plastic bag. Which probably confirmed in her mind that he was wrong in the head. But she was kind enough to keep on listening, tutting in sympathy at his predicament.

She was holding his hands comfortingly towards the end, and murmuring, "I'm sure everything will work out fine. Really, sweetheart. See?"

Evening was falling for the hundredth time as he went off along the street. Malcolm walked to Rembrandtsplein, and had a last meal gazing out across the leafy, busy square.

Watched people going by leading small children by the hand. Saw elderly couples smiling gently as they ambled through the lamplit dusk. Four tourists sat down at a table nearby his, and started to discuss what they were going to do tomorrow.

Malcolm headed back towards *Matt Black*. Pressed his way to the front, and then just stood there numbly. PVC were playing as exuberantly as ever. All their friends in the audience were going wild. Except Maya and her boyfriend, who were wrapped around each other, kissing fiercely.

And – though almost everyone in here was standing on the spot – it seemed to Malcolm that they were all moving forwards.

They were moving forwards towards other nights like this and different ones completely. They were moving forwards towards daybreaks by the thousand. Towards triumphs, large and minor. And disasters, large and minor. Happy days and disappointments. Tragedies and moments to be treasured. Times they were so bored they could not even move, and other days they got so bored they did something completely crazy.

They were all moving towards tomorrow, in other words.

And it was as though they were all riding on a bright, loud, bustling train, and he was watching them recede from the edge of a deserted platform.

Long before the band had finished, Malcolm put his coat on and went back outside. He thrust his hands deep in his pockets and tucked down his head. And just walked, away from the city centre.

He went by big rococo wall clocks, and by windows full of watches, and by ancient churches with high bell-towers, and he kept on going, feeling time itself crumble to grey ash around him like a smoked-out cigarette, listening for a peal of chimes he knew would never come ...

The Cure

I thought it was her, the woman who opened the door. She was old enough, and looked right, in her flowing, floral print clothes, with her white hair in a bun and her small, golden-rimmed spectacles. And the way she looked me up and down...

Her pale blue eyes seemed to take in everything at once. The crow's feet creases of pain around my eyes and mouth. And the way that the radiation and the chemotherapy had robbed me – at thirty-two – of nearly all my hair. The fact that I no longer properly filled out my clothes.

Her gaze lingered on my own eyes for longer than was polite. Perhaps taking in the awful fear that I saw every morning in the mirror.

I had just six weeks. If that.

Neither of us was saying anything, right at the moment. So I broke the impasse with a hasty, "Madame Celeste?"

She gave a small, tight smile. Shook her head. And answered, "I am her translator and assistant. Please come through. The fee is fifty pounds."

Just an ordinary little maisonette in a quiet suburb. Just a handbill I'd had thrust between my barely-willing fingers on the street. *Madame Celeste, faith-healer. Thousands of satisfied clients. Will cure all ills.*

Silly. No, amend that – quite ridiculous. But when you're thirty-two and you have just six weeks left ... if that ... you'll try anything.

She was younger than I was, which took me aback. In her mid-twenties, and slender, and quite pretty. Sitting on a breakfast stool in a perfectly ordinary fitted kitchen-diner, dressed in jeans and a white T-shirt and swinging her bare feet. Of what nationality? It was impossible to tell. Dark, certainly. But she could have been Latin American, or from the Indian subcontinent, Turkish, Kurdish, or even a gypsy. Strange, how we try to pigeonhole people the moment we see them. And even stranger, these days, just how difficult that is. Human beings do not fit into neat categories quite as simply as they used to.

She glanced up at me – her irises were deep black. Flashed me a very white ... and reassuring? ... smile. Then turned her attention to her assistant. They ducked heads together and conversed in whispers. It was obviously a foreign tongue, but one that I could not make out. I felt nervous and awkward, so I looked around the room.

There was not so much as a small crucifix. What had I been expecting?

More than this. More than laminated surfaces and tiles and a waffle-maker.

A faith-healer? Of what faith?

"Do you have the money?" the assistant asked, bringing my head back round.

They were both looking at me now.

I handed it over.

"Please step forward, within reach. She has to touch you."

Didn't they want me to tell them what was wrong? The cancer that had started in my liver and then spread like...

Like...?

Like nothing else in the world spreads. No similes. No metaphors. The worst word in the English language has to be 'malignant'.

I took an awkward three steps, still feeling perfectly ridiculous. Sweat was running down my upper lip. I almost flinched when Madame Celeste reached out, suddenly remembering stories about healers in South America who plunged their hands into their patients and pulled tumours out. All that she did, though, was brush her palm across my stomach. Then her arm withdrew, she looked away.

The smile on her assistant's face grew slightly broader. And she informed me, "You're done."

*

Before the diagnosis I'd have thrown a fit. Except, before the diagnosis, I'd have thrown away the handbill, thought of anyone who kept it and visited 'Madame Celeste' as a feeble-minded dunce.

I'd not only try anything by now, though. I'd accept anything, as well. I didn't let out so much as a grunt at being cheated, since what difference did it make. They could keep the fifty. I just turned around, and went home.

There was no pain at all, over the next few days. By the end of the week, I realised that I had gained a little weight again, and some of my hair was coming back. And the fear in the eyes was not as terrible as it had been before. As though my eyes knew something that the rest of me did not.

X-rays and an MRI confirmed it.

"It's complete remission!" the consultant beamed, as though he'd had something to do with it. "You must be extremely pleased."

Did he specialise in understatement?

I went to my favourite bar and drank a lot, then realised I had someone to thank.

*

It was still a perfectly ordinary maisonette. Still a perfectly ordinary kitchen-diner. She was with another client, though she didn't seem to mind me standing there and watching.

I was sure I recognised him, from the hospital. A very old man in a wheelchair, with his equally old wife. Even being seated seemed a hardship to him. He was almost doubled over, his face twisted up with pain and effort. His breathing was wheezy and uneven. And how long did *this* one have? Not even my original six weeks, I imagined.

His wife's face was completely blank, as though she had already lost him.

The five notes were handed over. Madame Celeste did the exact same thing, except her palm went slightly higher up this time.

The wife obviously wanted to say something, protest, when she realised it was over. Then she noticed me, standing there by the door.

And there must have been something in my expression. She simply turned the wheelchair around, with some difficulty, and went on her way.

Madame Celeste and her assistant smiled at me, and then conferred, the same way they had last time.

"Is there something else wrong?" I was asked.

"I just ... I had to ..."

"Yes – we know."

"If there's any way that I can ..."

"It was a service that you paid for. Madame Celeste does not expect any gifts, gratuities, or thanks."

"How can I *not* thank her?" I came back, rather astonished.

But all the assistant did was glance at her wristwatch.

"If you'll excuse us, we have another client due in a few minutes. We're extremely busy here, you know."

*

I began to notice it over the next couple of weeks. I was busy as all hell myself, having returned to my office job. But the adverts and the handbills and the cards pushed through my letter box began to impinge on my consciousness, at last. Dozens of them, in the classified section of the local paper. Dozens more, letting you know of their presence by means of cards in newsagents windows, even in phone boxes next to BUSTY BLONDE 18 YEAR OLD SEEKS FUN. Madame Celeste was far from alone.

Dozens?

There were *thousands* like her, just in my neck of the woods. God knew how many thousand right across the country. And I began thinking to myself – there's a whole new religion going on here.

Either that, or a very old one.

Life never quite returns to normal after something like I'd been through. You can do the same things as you used to, go to the same places, entertain yourself in the same ways. But there's always a brittle feeling to everything, a jaggedness that was never there before. You feel very slightly manic, deep down, and that is not pleasant. But considering the alternative...

It was now five and a half weeks since I'd visited Madame Celeste. In a few more days, I realised – and I smiled – I'd have been no more of this world. My sentence had been commuted. The phone had rung, and it had been the Governor on the other end. That felt good. My inner mania faded slightly.

I was due one final check-up at out-patients. I was walking from the bus stop to the hospital, a sunny day. I reached the gates.

There was the old man I'd seen in the kitchen-diner.

He was no longer in his wheelchair. He was standing perfectly upright, and seemed to have gained several pounds. His face was not so withered. It was still screwed up with pain, though.

He was crying uncontrollably, his shoulder against the gate post.

I went up to him, astonished. Asked, "Are you all right?"

His tear-filled eyes came a slit open, and he peered at me, not seeming to recognise me at all. His mouth moved. A sound came out, but he was so choked up with crying it was just that.

So he tried again. One word. Was it 'horrible'?

His eyelids screwed up tightly, and remained like that this time.

"Do you need any help? Where's your wife?"

But all he did was shake his head, and then start crying even harder, quite forgetting I was there.

He was senile, I decided. Madame Celeste had been able to get him out of his chair, but curing his mind seemed beyond her.

I went on my way.

*

Six weeks exactly. I woke up. Another sunny day. Chinks of golden light pouring through my curtains.

Some of them were touching me. My left hand and shoulder. My bare chest.

I'd come wide awake but, oddly, I couldn't seem to feel them. Couldn't detect any warmth. The rays of sunlight looked ... peculiar. They'd never appeared oppressive before. Never made me want to shy away.

I didn't seem to be breathing properly. Felt quite choked. As though the air was full of heavy dust.

Oh God, what was wrong now? I pulled on a robe, went down, and made some breakfast.

The milk smelled sour, so I threw it out. But the coffee smelled sour too. And tasted of nothing.

The toast and butter seemed to have the consistency of sponge and axle-grease.

Was I coming down with the flu?

I switched on the radio. The music jarred my ears. I turned it off.

My breathing was still laboured.

*

Everything I tried to eat tasted of nothing. The same with drink. I couldn't listen to music at all. Sunlight left me, in every sense, cold. I watched my favourite sitcom that evening, and didn't laugh.

I woke up the next morning and my breathing was *still* laboured.

Flowers I passed by had no smell. Even young women on the tube into work ... aroused no interest in me.

The flu? Or even M.E.? Or a side-effect of the chemo? I went to my GP. Who could find nothing.

Then it started dawning on me. Had the cancer come back?

My consultant saw me again quickly enough, as concerned as I was. But I was still clear.

"You came very close to dying," he told me. "Sometimes, there can be quite a strong psychological backlash."

He suggested I give Prozac a try.

I tried it for a while. It did absolutely nothing. Then, I threw the tablets away and tried getting very drunk instead.

It was all the badness of inebria, with none of the good. My head swam and I felt sick, and I finally was, very messily. But with none of the loose happiness that usually precedes that, none of the unfettered joy or false invulnerability.

I'd never tried drugs. No, correct that, I had. Prozac. Why should anything bought on a street corner work any better?

What was the solution here? There had to be a cure for this.

*

I had trouble getting to sleep, and I loathed waking up. Because it was always the same.

My breathing? It was as though I were trying to breathe underground. As though I had been buried and...

And it had started six weeks after seeing Madame Celeste. Possibly on the exact day I had been supposed to –

Stop that! Stop that utter nonsense! You're a rational human being, and if you're actually going to start entertaining notions of some price to be paid. Some Faustian hocus-pocus...!

But then I remembered what the old man had said, leaning against the gate-post, half-drowning in his own tears. What he *might* have said.

'Horrible'.

It had just been bad, to start with. Just like feeling ... out of sorts. But as one day overtook the next...

It wasn't that it got worse. It just simply didn't change.

How long now? A fortnight?

I hadn't smiled. I hadn't tasted anything. Felt anything. Even taken a good deep clean breath. Everything seemed bled of colour. Even during the chemo, I'd had nothing quite like that. Maybe I was going mad.

Was there *anything* that I could find enjoyment in?

I realised there might be. But even that realisation didn't make me crack a smile.

I'd been badly ill, quite visibly so. And so it had been a while.

There was this girl at work, though, who'd seemed interested in me in the past. I took her to a bar that evening, made no secret of the fact that I was trying to get her drunk.

I was not good company, and was aware of that. But maybe she took the darkness of my mood as something dangerous and exciting.

Whatever, we were back at her place just as the sun set.

And it wasn't that I couldn't. All the reflexes were still in place. It was that ... it made me feel nothing.

Nothing except envy. Her head was thrown back, her eyelids half-closed in that fluttery way, her lips wet and parted. She was making little groans.

I was still trying to draw a proper breath, as I had been doing for two weeks now.

I simply stopped, half way through it. Rolled off the bed and started pulling my clothes back on.

She was awfully drunk. She swore at me. Said something about it being a little late to find out I was gay.

Something hit the door, thrown hard, as I went through it.

How did that make me feel?

Guess.

*

I had to make my way on foot, without a map, and so it took more than two hours before I found the maisonette again. Most of the windows around me were dark, up and down the ordinary street. Including hers.

I banged on the door until the older woman answered.

She was in a nightrobe, her hair askew, and looked alarmed to see me.

"What did she do to me?" I yelled.

"Would you please keep your voice down. Do you know what time it is?"

"What did that bitch *do* to me?"

"Exactly what you wanted."

"What I – ?"

"You had six weeks left. You wanted to go beyond that. So you have."

"So I ..."

"Not as you were before, though. Still alive or not, your time is up."

And, for the first time since that awful morning, my mouth formed a smile. But it was suspicion and wryness only, no humour at all.

"What are you telling me? That she is Mephistopheles, and she saved my life, and now she's got my soul or something?"

The woman's head gave a tiny shake. "No, precisely the opposite. Quite a while ago, your kind made a deal with my employer. An agreement, if you will. A covenant. You would live in this place for a period of time, worship her, and try to avoid evil. After that, you'd be looked after for the rest of eternity. But it's not simply that you do not believe in that these days. It's you don't even *want* it. You just want to stay here. Whatever it takes. Whosoever offers it.

"Do you realise how hurtful she finds that? So many of you going back on your word, trying to cheat her with cheap tricks? Hundreds like you come here every week. And, like you, they're still around. If that's what you want, well, that's what she'll now give you."

At that point, a younger female voice started calling out from the back, in that same peculiar language I had overheard before. The assistant turned her head and answered similarly.

I was still trying to understand what she'd just told me. Was she seriously suggesting that I'd...?

Broken some kind of contract? With...?

My confusion started turning into renewed anger.

"What *language* is that you're speaking?" I burst out, louder than ever.

She stopped then, and looked back at me pointedly.

"The language of the Covenant," she told me. "Aramaic."

And she slammed the door shut in my slack, cold face.

A Matter Of Avoiding Crowds

Really knowing your way around central London, on foot, is a matter of avoiding crowds. Frank Lancey knew this, and had got it down to a fine art.

If you're coming down Charing Cross Road, for instance, and you want to get to Leicester Square you're better cutting along the bottom edge of Chinatown than pushing your way through the seething mass outside the Hippodrome. If you want to get from Tottenham Court Road to Selfridges department store, then you'll do it in half the time by using Mortimer and Wigmore Streets, rather than shuffling with the shoppers and the tourists along Oxford Street itself.

Frank had been lucky enough, after the divorce, to keep hold of the little flat in the purpose-built block at the end of Gerrard Street. Had lived there on his own for two years now. Loved to walk – it was one of the few things he did enjoy. And knew the footways of the city just as thoroughly as a London cabbie knows the roads.

It was late evening, a Wednesday. He had just been out for a long stroll. Down Shaftesbury Avenue. Off at Great Windmill Street to avoid the scrums that gathered at the traffic lights on Piccadilly Circus. Left onto Brewer Street. Across Regent Street. Vigo, then Burlington Gardens. Up Old Bond Street. Along Oxford Street itself, the shops all shut now. Then a quick cut left to Cavendish Square to avoid Oxford Circus. Across Regent Street a second time. Market Place, Eastcastle Street, then home along Wardour.

The phone started ringing while he unlocked his front door. The answering machine cut in, though, before he could reach it.

"Hello, Frank?"

It was Margaret. The first time he'd heard from her in over a year.

"Hello, Frank, are you there? Obviously not. It's me. Thought I'd just phone and see how you are. David and I split up a week ago, but that doesn't mean that I've got an ulterior motive. It's just, we meant a lot to each other once, and I just wanted to make sure you're all right. Maybe we can get together sometime for a friendly drink? Same number. Call me when you can."

The line went dead, without her even saying 'bye'.

Frank played the message through twice, and then went to hang away his raincoat before coming back and playing it three times more. He couldn't even tell, from the tone of her voice, what her emotional state was. She didn't sound hostile, but did not sound friendly either, despite the suggestion of a meeting.

She did not appear upset, needy, nor even condescending. Her tone was completely neutral. An impenetrable flatness.

He felt glad that she and David had split up, though. David was younger than he was, fitter, better-off and better-looking. So, she didn't deserve him.

Frank muttered an oath under his breath, deleted the message, and then fetched himself a beer and settled down in front of the TV.

The crowds passing through Chinatown's main thoroughfare set up a continuous murmuring beyond his window. But he had got so used to that, he didn't even notice it at all.

*

If you want to get from Liberty's to John Lewis, then you don't go up to Oxford Circus and turn left, you take Hanover Street and cut across Hanover Square.

William IV Street is the only sane way to get to the St. Martin's Lane end of Trafalgar Square if you're coming along The Strand.

Frank was office manager for a small law firm situated just behind the University College of London, and so the walk each morning was an easy one. Through Soho up Frith Street. Across Oxford Street. Rathbone Place, Charlotte Street. Right at Grafton Way and across the lights – an irritating wait – on Tottenham Court Road. Sometimes he would vary it by turning right on Maple Street instead.

He always lunched at the same place – Guido's, one of those Italian-run coffee and sandwich shops which are London's equivalent of New York deli-diners. All the tables were formica-topped, and the coffee-machine hissed like an injured beast several times a minute. The front window was invariably misted-up. The people walking past it? You could barely make them out.

Apart from a couple of young secretaries who were always busy, he was the only person in the building who was not a lawyer. And was generally talked down to because of that fact. Or at least, that was how it felt.

He was usually tired when he got home, though not from overwork. Rather, from the tedium of the day, the fact that he had been in his job twenty years too long. Still, it paid well, allowing him to afford this place. And a walk always cleared his head and left him feeling better.

Newport Street. Right onto St. Martin's Lane. Brydges Place – so narrow you could be unlucky if there was a group of people travelling the other way. But there wasn't this evening. Chandos Place. Then left again onto Wellington which ran up onto Bow Street which joined Upper Shaftesbury Avenue. Which, using Monmouth to dodge the snarling mess that was Cambridge Circus, took him home.

A car door slammed to his left just as he passed Shelton Street. He glanced around to see a well-dressed Middle Eastern man helping a woman out of a top-of-the-range silver Mercedes

And thought for a moment that he was staring at Margaret. She was the same height and shape, had the same auburn hair worn piled-up for the evening. But it wasn't her. He walked the rest of the way to his front door looking neither left nor right.

There were two messages on his machine when he got in this time. The first was another from guess who?

"Me again. I see you haven't bothered to return my call. Well this is the last time I'm trying, out of sheer decency's sake. If you'd ever bothered to do *anything*, perhaps I wouldn't have needed someone else."

It did not need re-playing, he decided, since the tone was clear enough.

The second?

"Frank, hi? This is Chris – as in Chris and Jean? It kind of occurred to us a short while back that we haven't seen you in ages. Sorry about that, mate – you know how awkward these things are. But we were thinking – how'd you like to come around for dinner? Catch up on each other's news, that kind of thing? Again, sorry it's been so long, but we thought it's a shame to lose touch completely because of ... you know, what happened with Maggie. Love to see you. Look forward to your call. If you haven't kept our number then it's – "

Frank reached down and skipped the message to the end.

Chris and Jean had been friends back when he had been part of a couple. They used to live in a big, cheap housing association flat in Bloomsbury – ten minutes walk from here. But had decided they wanted a house and kids some eight years back, and had moved to Mill Hill.

He had only visited them once since the break-up, about a month after Margaret had decamped. And had hated the whole experience. Loathed taking a tube train all the way north to the outer suburbs. Despised the rows of same-looking, Thirties-built, semi-detached houses set on measurably parallel streets.

(If you're trying to get to Covent Garden Piazza from the west, then you're better cutting down one of the alleyways to Floral Street than sticking to Long Acre).

And, worst of all, he'd felt entirely disembowelled by the fact that they were still a happy couple. Glances and quick smiles had passed between them all the while that he was there.

'We're not going to end up *that* way', each wordless exchange said.

He'd made his excuses and got out of there as soon as he was able. Hadn't even bothered to ride the infernal train the whole way back to Leicester Square. Got off at Warren Street, three stops short, instead.

Fitzroy Square. Cleveland Street. Newman Street. Across Oxford Street. Great Chapel Street. Dean Street. Across Shaftesbury Avenue. Home –

All the people he'd known socially were exactly the same. He had only ever known them as part of a couple; they were couples too.

They had all been Margaret's friends originally, it had occurred to him some time ago.

Frank erased both messages.

He got himself another bottle of beer from the fridge, but didn't switch the TV on when he sat down this time.

Just sat there, thinking about the woman stepping out of the big, expensive Mercedes. Of how much she'd looked like Margaret.

Then he thought about how physically beautiful Margaret had been ... still was? And how wonderful it had felt to be in bed with her, almost right up to the end.

It was as though all that had been experienced by someone else entirely. In a wholly different body, in another place and time. He could only seem to recall it from an impossible distance.

After an extended while – and this was unusual – a noise made him look up. At first, he thought that it was just the wind making it, getting down a gap in the walls or up along a waste-pipe. But no, it was more solid than that.

A scratching noise. An even scrabbling.

A rat, he realised at last, somewhere in the brickwork around him.

He considered calling the building's superintendent, but then decided against it.

Thought about the rat instead. Cutting under floors. Skimming over ceilings. Using pipes and vents and flues as short-cuts.

Spending a whole busy life avoiding being seen.

*

If you're heading down from Centre Point in the direction of the theatres, then the left side of the street is invariably less crowded than the right.

Jermyn Street will take you the whole way from St. James' to the Haymarket without touching Piccadilly once.

If you don't know about and use South Molton Street – wholly pedestrianised – then you don't know your way around the centre of town at all.

Carnaby Street is closed to traffic too. But crowded.

*

Waxman Court?

He stopped and gazed at the street sign, then down the narrow lane.

There was a *Flaxman* Court off Wardour Street, but it was a dead-end, taking you nowhere. And yet here he was on Greek Street, which he'd walked perhaps a thousand times. And ... how long had he lived just down from Soho? ... he was peering down a street he'd never noticed until now.

It was a Saturday evening, his least favourite time of the week. Normally he stayed indoors, but the silence of his living room had finally driven him out. Not even the rat had come back to keep him company.

Where'd it gone? Where exactly *did* rats go when you couldn't hear them?

Saturday evening. Properly, Saturday night. It was practically impossible to dodge the crowds. Great, mixed gaggles of friends laughed and yelled and staggered. Girls clattered by in tight-knit packs, clad in the briefest of dresses, all oblivious to the cold.

Couples went past arm in arm, ambling or quickly.

A lot of these people knew the same short-cuts as he did.

Waxman Court.

How had he missed it all this time?

Frank gazed its length suspiciously.

The lane was not wide enough to even allow traffic down it. Had a pitted, cobbled surface, with a narrow row of paving stones on either side. Was dimly-lit, the lamp-posts far apart, their bulbs dull ochre. He knew that he had to be careful in such places these days. Junkies had invaded Soho quite a few years back, and lay in wait for people along thoroughfares like this.

But the street was empty of tonight's annoying throngs. And he wondered where it led.

It took him, after several bends, to a sharp right turn onto ... Brutal Place?

There was a Bru*ton* Place in Mayfair. But this couldn't be it – he hadn't so much as crossed over Regent Street as yet. Had some kids been tampering with the signs?

When he reached the next street – wider, and far better lit – he swallowed hard and stared round with bewilderment. Since he certainly now knew where he was. This was North Audley Street.

But *couldn't* be.

He hadn't been walking that long, for a start. And he had *definitely* not crossed the four crammed lanes of Regent Street, which he needed to, to get here.

He walked the hundred yards or so to the top, his head swimming. And yes – he was on Oxford Street now, Marble Arch and Hyde Park just a couple of blocks away. So this really was North Audley.

Perhaps his mind had been wandering and he'd lost track of time and location, he considered. Maybe he'd simply ... got lost?

These things did happen. Although never – until now – to him.

It was better that he went home by the more conventional routes. He did not feel exactly at his best, right at this moment. Seemed confused, his mind detached and slightly dizzy.

A wind blew up suddenly, more than a touch of damp in it. Frank tucked his chin down against his coat collar, made his lone way along Oxford Street towards the bright lights that were gleaming in the distance. But he didn't feel wholly comfortable doing so. Felt vulnerable out here.

With the stores all shut, grilles down across most of them, there was no reason for the Saturday night revellers to come this way. The farther you got from Marble Arch tube station, the less people were about. Which normally would have suited him fine. Except that some worse elements came here at night-time, drawn in by the vacuum.

The sudden loud report of smashing glass proved the point. Walking closer, Frank could see a cluster of hunched people up ahead of him. They were ragged, shapeless, looked like beggars. And – several of them were shouting obscenely – all seemed aggressively drunk.

There were about ten of them. Perhaps a dozen.

Another empty bottle hurtled through the air and smashed against the far kerb, spraying fragments.

Which meant that simply crossing the street wouldn't totally avoid them. And he saw that one of them had a big, snarling dog, which he was holding by the collar.

The next decision was almost reflexive – Frank cut right down Gilbert Street rather than continue onwards.

And came to a second halt at the corner of another unfamiliar, narrow lane.

Hide Street.

There was a *Hinde* Street, he knew. But it was north of Selfridges, not south.

It appeared to take him in the right direction, though. And so he took it.

And emerged, within a few minutes, on Leicester Square itself.

Which was utterly *impossible*.

Frank turned on the spot three times, trying to understand how he had wound up here. Each time that he turned round, he got jostled.

He was on the north side of the square – the broad *terrazzo* – and it was crowded to bursting point. Eager, smiling people poured around him in an endless flow, as though from a machine used for creating vast mobs, its 'off' button broken. Buskers howled and piped and strummed above the waves of chatter. Massive neon lights flashed over cinemas and nightclubs, swanky bars.

How long had he spent avoiding areas like this?

And then, somehow, he saw her, coming through the mob towards him. She was with three other people.

Margaret was just as beautiful as he'd ever remembered her, and done up to the nines. He didn't even recognise that purple sequinned dress.

The other couple were Chris and Jean, who hadn't changed at all since he'd last seen them.

And the fourth?

Another man. Partnering Margaret. Just as tall and handsome as David had been. But not David.

Already? So soon? How did anyone's life move quite that fast?

She was hanging onto his elbow. Her face was close to his, and she was chattering and laughing.

He was smiling back, his eyes on her pale blue ones.

Frank ... was staring directly at her too. If she'd only once look up, then she would see him.

She did not, despite the fact that she was getting ever closer. She would simply bump into him at this rate, and then be startled and – perhaps – embarrassed.

He tried to imagine it. How he'd feel being introduced to this good-looking stranger.

His stomach began to tighten.

The opening to Hide Street was still behind him. How appropriate. He ducked back into it.

Hide Street met a junction at something called Living Street – there was a *Livonia* Street. Which in turn gave way to Lost and Found Road. Shouldn't that be *Rose and Crown Road*?

Which in turn...

He kept on going for half an hour, realising increasingly this simply was not right. He'd never heard of any of these new streets he was walking down. And they were all of the same width and appearance.

There was something even stranger, though.

All of them were bounded in by old featureless walls, so high that he could not make out a roof, even a gutter. He had not passed by a single door, a porch, a window in how long by now? Not a single frontage. There was not so much as a small poster or graffiti daub on the evenly-weathered brickwork.

And, despite there being no yellow lines along the kerbs, there wasn't even so much as a chained bicycle parked.

In all this time, he'd passed no one. Which was the greatest impossibility of all. You couldn't walk around town for this long on a Saturday night and not see another living soul, however obscure the route you took.

Frank trailed to a halt, and realised that he couldn't even hear the distant thrum of traffic.

Where on earth had he wound up?

He could now hear something else, though.

Very faintly, through the nearest wall, he thought he could make out a group of people, chattering excitedly and laughing against a background of crockery and cutlery noises. Was he at the back of a restaurant? Or perhaps behind someone's home?

He knew that he was on a lane called Betterthan now – it ought to be Betterton. Walked up to the next junction, praying that it was a street he recognised. He still had to be in Soho, since he'd crossed no major thoroughfare. Though he remembered how the first two routes had taken him to places which he shouldn't have wound up in.

Buried Place.

There was a Bury Place near the British Museum, but this wasn't it.

He backtracked till he could hear the voices again.

There were perhaps eight people on the far side of the wall. Enjoying an evening out or a dinner party, just like he and Margaret had once done. He found it hard to make out individual words – several people were speaking at once, their tones delighted.

It seemed a wonderful evening, on the far side of the wall.

And he didn't quite know what to do, but was sure of one thing. For the very first time in London, he was well and truly, deeply lost. And beginning, now, to panic.

So he started yelling to them. Could they help him? Could they tell him where he was?

And, when that got no response, he began actually slamming on the brickwork with his fists.

The chatter faded to a halt.

"Did you just hear anything? What was that?"

"Perhaps something in the wall," replied a man's voice.

One of the women gave a startled yip.

"Don't worry," came the same man's fluid tones. "Whatever it is, it can't get in here."

The chatter resumed a moment later, even busier than before.

And did not stop, however hard Frank thumped and yelled.

Went on and on, without him.

*

He was forced to give it up, in the end. Blood was leaking out of the fine creases in his fists. The flesh was turning purple.

He turned and slumped against the brickwork, in pain and exhausted.

It was when his eyelids finally came open that he realised he was being watched.

A few yards off along the worn cobbles, two small, very bright eyes were peering at him. He could make out the grey silhouette of a body behind them, little more than a foot tall.

It was a rat ... the same rat from his apartment? And was standing on its hind legs, with its smaller front paws drawn up to its chest. Its nose twitched, its long whiskers shivering. But it was not studying him in any kind of troubled or malicious fashion.

Where *did* rats go when you couldn't hear them?

After a long while, Frank pushed himself away from the wall, took a step towards the creature. It didn't budge, although its nose lifted a slight shade higher.

When he took a second step, though, it dropped to all fours and turned around. Scuttled away to the corner of Buried Place.

Where it stopped in the act of turning right. Glanced back at him across one slicked-down shoulder.

Frank looked at it carefully, taking in a slow, deep breath. It seemed to know its way round here.

Then followed.

Non-Existent Cats

This, as the title already tells you, is all about cats that aren't there. And by 'cats', I mean the small domestic kind, not big lions and other stuff, or cool, jazz-type people.

Are you with me so far? Good.

Anyway, it started like this. The phone went, about nine in the morning. I was half way into my pants, the store opening at ten, and had to hop over to answer it. And when I pick it up I hear like, "*Lenn-iieee!*"

My name's Leonard Melnic, by the way. Just Len to my friends. My girlfriend's the only person that I let call me 'Lenny' since, like what, I'm still going to have people call me Lenny when I'm one hundred years old or something? I'm twenty four, and am into comic books and garage music and all kind of films, except sub-titled ones. I have this party trick where I play bongos and eat a whole Big Mac at the same time – *you* try it. Not so easy, huh? And I work at that big alternative bookstore on Union, *Rolling Paper*.

My girlfriend's Megan, and she's only – erm – eighteen, and a Goth. Which means she has long, very straight dark hair with purple streaks in it, and is into S&M clothes and imagery, though not the reality. We tried a spanking session once, at *her* insistence, and she didn't speak to me for practically a whole week.

So anyway, "*Lenn-iieee!*"

And it's Megan, which surprises me since she only works at the beauty parlour in the afternoon and is usually right out of it until at least ten thirty.

"Hey, what's up?"

"Get over here, *please*!"

"Are you all right?"

"Of course not! There's been a cat in my room! I got up to pee, and there were scratches on the furniture!"

So I look at my watch. Megan's is ten minutes away. The store? Twenty, in the other direction.

"Is it still there?"

"That's what I want you to find out!"

And then she starts making this whimpering noise that simply breaks my heart.

The strange thing about Megan, see, is that even though she's a Goth and into all kinds of witchy stuff like candles and amulets and Tolkein posters, she just can't stand cats. In the first place, they give her the creeps. And in the second, she's allergic to them.

I don't like them either. They're all sniffy, like some fox who won't give you the time of day. And they have this thing where they jump in your lap and you try to get them off, and they don't want to move and dig their claws in. Yow! But I'm not scared of them the way Megan is. So I get over there.

I go up the staircase to her third floor walk-up, and when I knock on the door I hear this thump, like someone jumping around. And the door comes open a few seconds later, and there's Megan standing there, looking cute in just her scanties, but looking pretty wide-eyed and scared with it.

"What was that noise?" I ask her.

"I was standing on the bed."

"I thought that was for mice? What, like a cat can't climb up on a bed?"

"Oh, shut up, stupid! Just get in here!" And she yanks me inside, strong despite the fact she's pretty tiny. "*Look* for the damn thing!"

So I begin The Great Cat Hunt. Megan hops back on the bed, teetering around and looking foxier than ever. And she keeps trying to direct me, going, "over there, look behind that", and such-like. But who's doing the work here, me or her?

All I find of interest, in the end, is a pile of old teen romance mags in the bottom of a closet, and a big purple vibrator that I've never seen before. And Megan jumps off the bed and snatches it out of my hand and puts it away at that point, so she's obviously calmed down a little.

"There's nothing here," I tell her, still smirking a bit about the vibrator and the way she's looking flushed. "It probably went out through the window."

"That's the crazy thing!" she wails now. "There weren't any windows open! How could the thing get in *or* out?"

So I ask her to show me the scratches. And there they are, clear as day, on two of the legs of her rickety dining table and one of the chairs. I bend down and inspect them carefully. And finally, I purse my lips.

"Hmm, it looks like a cat." I hope that my tone sounds impressive. "Do you think it could be Mr. Paws?"

But Megan sounds less than overwhelmed by my brilliant deduction.

Fortunately for her, there are no cats in her building since pets aren't allowed. But if you look out her kitchen window into the space out back, you can usually see a big fat tabby sitting on the first floor window ledge of the building behind this one. He belongs to an old lady, and is the laziest cat you've ever seen, only ever moving himself at meal-times. We looked out the window now, and there he was, a rotund ball of fur.

Mr. Paws couldn't climb onto a cinderblock, let alone up here.

So we're both pretty puzzled. I do my best to calm her down, which involves kidding her a lot and tickling her. And the fact that she's still in her underwear starts to get to both of us.

But I'm already late at the store. I swear it, man, this Protestant Work Ethic shit? It's gonna be the death of me.

*

Nine-thirty the next morning, the phone goes again.

"*Lenn-iiee!*"

And I think 'oh fuck'.

"My *curtains* are shredded! I think it's still hiding in here!"

But I know perfectly well it isn't. Megan's place isn't that big, and I searched every square inch of it. I remind her of that, getting rather annoyed while I do so.

"If I come round there, I'm going to be late again, and Chan'll have my guts!"

"You're a mean son-of-a-bitch!" she tells me. And then she hangs up.

I didn't see or hear from her the whole day.

The *next* morning at nine-thirty?

Yep, you guessed it.

"*Pleeease!*"

So I get round there. Megan's pretty shaken-up, all trembly, by this time. And yes, her curtains are shredded up pretty badly. So I try to think this through.

"Cats usually leave a smell," I tell her. "But there isn't one. Can you find any fur?"

We looked, and didn't.

"You could try, like, sprinkling talcum powder on the floor, seeing if it leaves any paw marks?"

But she's too freaked to get her head round anything sensible right now, and she keeps clinging on to me, and this time we do end up making out, at ten-fifteen in the morning. Just call that striking a blow for the ordinary working man.

Some time mid-afternoon, Megan shows up in the store and says, "I want some books on ghosts."

"Say what?"

"It's a ghost-cat. It's the only thing it can be. And I want a book on exorcisms too."

"Don't priests do that?"

"God, Lenny. You know I'm not religious."

So she ends up buying three volumes, using my discount. And when she's gone, Chan Park, the store's joint-owner, comes sauntering across to me with the usual supercilious look on his face.

Now Chan's a pretty stylish-looking dude, always dressed in leather, with a little moustache and goatee beard that I have to admit look pretty cool on a Korean. And he's very smart, and reads a lot of heavy non-fiction stuff. But he does have airs and graces. Yeah right, like he thinks nobody knows he drops so many E's at the weekend he'd end up humping Genghis Khan if Genghis Khan smiled at him nicely.

"So, Leonard," he says. "It seems your barely legal girlfriend has wigged out completely."

Which is designed to annoy me and does, since he's always making snide remarks about Megan's age. But I don't respond. In the first place, I'm already in the dog-house for the second late-show in a week. And in the second, I have this theory by now, and maybe Chan's the right person to try it out on.

I explain what's been going on, and he keeps looking at me like I'm on something.

"Do you agree with her, about the ghost stuff?"

"No, man. She's a Goth, and Goths believe in that shit. What I think, see, is that there's this kind of alternate world, just like ours but different, and – "

"Leonard?" Chan just snaps. "Would you spare me all the Star Trek bullshit? Yes, okay I'll admit, quantum theory does point to the probability of separate planes of existence. But they're kept apart, quite strongly I'd imagine. I'd suggest it would take the force of something like a black hole to break through. And do you think a fucking cat would go to all that trouble just to shred your little girlfriend's curtains?"

I had to admit that didn't sound too likely.

"But I'll tell you what it might be, though."

And he's gone ever so slightly smirky now, so that I can't tell whether he's jerking my chain or not.

But he starts to tell me all about this dude called Professor Stephen Hawking. I think I saw him on the TV once – he's the guy who talks funny, right? And apparently, this guy has figured out how much the entire galaxy weighs –

"How did he do *that*? I mean, that's *impossible!*"

Chan rolls his eyeballs up before continuing.

And has realised that there isn't enough mass – I think I've got this right – to create enough gravity to hold the whole fuck-wad together. So he gets this idea that there might be other stuff out there called Dark Matter, which we can't see or touch. And there are other scientists who are looking for it now, and some of them even think they've found some.

I almost burst in with *how?* again, but my head's throbbing a little and I'm waiting for Chan to get to the point.

"Think about this." And he's grinning openly by now. "If there is Dark Matter, why should it just be like dust, floating in space? I'm made of matter. So are you. So's that delivery you haven't unpacked yet."

"I guess so."

"And so, why shouldn't Dark Matter form real, even living objects? Like cats?"

And he walks off grinning like he's just made out with Brad Pitt *and* Brad Pitt's cloned twin brother.

I was pretty sure that he *was* mostly yanking my chain. But knowing Chan and the way he likes to air his knowledge, I was also pretty sure that that Dark Matter stuff was based in fact.

My head was still throbbing slightly by the time we closed up, and I thought about it all the way to Megan's. Matter that wasn't there, but was? Non-existent stuff that some egg-head could prove did exist? Wow, the world just kept on getting weirder, and science wasn't exactly helping matters any.

When Megan opened the door, there were, like, a hundred thousand candles lit up all behind her. And she was clutching a bible which she'd borrowed from the Baptist spinster two floors down.

"I am *never* going to get her off my back now," Megan complained. "She kept asking if I want to go to church."

Anyway, the whole point was – as you've probably guessed – she was about to perform an exorcism, and was waiting for yours truly to join in. I tried explaining to her about Dark Matter, but she didn't buy it, not a bit.

"Weighed the *galaxy?*" she kept on saying. "That's such total bullshit!"

So we did the whole Rod Steiger bit. No one's head span around. No one chucked. Nothing at all happened, except I practically set fire to my pants when I stepped backwards into a row of candles. But at the end of it, Megan had a strange, satisfied look on her face, calm like.

"It's gone," she told me. "I can feel things like that."

Like I keep on pointing out, she *is* a Goth.

I decided to do the noble, gentlemanly thing, though.

"Look, I'll stay over tonight, just to make sure everything's returned to normal."

"Sounds nice."

And she starts rubbing up against me, so I have to push her back a little.

"No! You know what'll happen if we do that. I'll fall flat asleep afterwards. I have to stay, like, focussed."

Typically of Megan, though, she doesn't let it go at that, and it doesn't take long before I succumb. But I force myself to get up straight away when we're done, since I have a duty to perform tonight. Think tough. Think steely. Think Clint Eastwood in that movie where he's protecting the President, 'The Bodyguard'. Shit, no, that's Kevin Costner.

"Coffee, wench," I command Megan.

And she honestly doesn't mind. She's got this special glow about her now.

"Are you really going to stay up all night?"

"I hope so, just to make sure. Have you got some ups?"

Of course she did. It's the way Goth chicks stay so thin.

Anyway, there I am at four in the morning, sitting at the foot of Megan's bed. And Megan's snoring really loudly – Jesus! And my eyelids are starting to get heavy, and I don't really want to take *another* up – I, you know, have my health to think of. So I force myself. Show true grit. Real, rigid determination.

'In The Line of Fire', *that's* the one.

And guess what, I did it. Stayed awake the whole way through till dawn. You didn't think I had it in me, did you?

So the daylight starts shining through Megan's thin, shredded curtains.

And there are huge parallel scratches on the plaster of the wall beneath them.

Megan goes berserk when she wakes up.

"You fell asleep! For God's sake!"

"No I didn't."

"You must have done!"

But I know what the truth is. And I'm realising something else as well. Not just that I didn't see anything. There wasn't a sound. And you'd have heard a scritching as the claws went down the plaster, at the very least.

So I keep thinking ... Dark Matter! Stuff that actually exists, but isn't there.

And the next thing, there's this awful noise from out back. Megan and I both rush to the kitchen window, just in time to see a gruesome sight.

The downstairs window of the block behind is open. And through it, we can see the old lady who owns Mr. Paws. Or *thought* she did. Because Mr. Paws is all over her face, scratching and yowling. And she's screaming her head off.

After a few seconds of this, Mr. Paws lets go and jumps out through the window, where he prowls around the little courtyard, his back arched, all snarly.

And this from a cat who wouldn't move a muscle if you stuck a knife up its fat ass.

"What's got *into* him?" Megan asks, her voice extremely quivery now.

"I don't know."

An ambulance came after a while. And then a couple of guys with long thick gloves, who still had a hell of a time getting Mr. Paws into a basket.

After that, everything just calmed down flat to normal.

Megan was still somewhat freaked, but if I was late for work again I knew that Chan would fire me.

I thought about it all day, though. And this is what I half-way figured. Look, it must be cool in some ways being a Dark Matter cat. You can move about and do stuff without anyone being able to stop you. Hell, if I was a Dark Matter Leonard Melnic –

Well, you get the picture.

But it must get pretty boring after a while. Like, wouldn't it be better to have an actual real body and be able to do realer stuff?

Where's the body come from though? Could Dark Matter and ... er ... Mattery Matter exist in the same place?

Mr. Paws?

And the way that he behaved? Well, it seemed to make sense that Dark Matter creatures would have a dark nature.

I didn't go back to Megan's that evening, because the idea freaked me out too much.

But at eight p.m., the phone goes.

*

"There's someone in here!"

"The cat?"

"No, a person! I can't see her! But she's in the bathroom, moving stuff around!"

"Fuck Megan, just get *out* of there, right now!"

I only begin wondering why Meg called the intruder 'she' after I've put the phone down. Since ... she couldn't see who it was, and intruders are usually 'he'.

Maybe she sensed something.

As I said at the beginning of this, it is ten minutes to Megan's. More like five if you're moving fast.

Twenty fucking minutes passed before I saw her shadowy figure coming down the street. Twenty god-almighty friggit minutes during which I paced and clenched and almost went insane.

So I throw open my window, and I'm about to ask her where she's been, when I see that there's a big bag thrown over her shoulder.

"You *packed*?"

She looks up at me, but I can't see her features.

"I've got some expensive stuff! I'm not insured, you know!"

"You fucking *packed*, with an intruder in your place?"

"Don't talk to me like that! I'm coming up!"

About half a minute later, I can hear her footsteps coming up the stairs, and I'm reaching for my doorknob –

*

And I'm still there now, with my hand half-way towards it, but not moving.

Megan's banging on the door, and saying the same things over and over. They started out whiney-bewildered, and then whiney-frightened. Now she's sounding whiney-cross.

"Lenn-iieee? Please! Let me in! Lenny, what are you *doing*?"

I'm not listening to the words any more. Just to the tone of her voice. Trying to detect something.

What?

Like ... sly. Deceptive.

Something ... just not right.

You see, I may not be any Professor Stephen Hawking, but I've figured out one thing for myself.

If there really are such things as non-existent cats, then a lot of them, without a doubt, have non-existent owners.

Yesterday, Upon The Stair

Though she doesn't know it, I've been living with a very nice and very pretty girl for well over a month now. That is the longest that I've stopped anywhere since I faded.

Her name is Katie Lewes. She has to be somewhere between twenty-two and twenty-five. No way of knowing for sure – such as her filling out a form containing her birthdate, for instance – has presented itself as yet. She does secretarial work for one of those small film production companies in Soho. And she's a veritable English rose.

I just noticed her in the street and began following her one day, though you could never call it 'stalking'. Stalkers want to threaten, to be noticed. I have faded and, therefore, cannot be.

In the first few weeks after it happened, I thought I had died, become a ghost. Wandered the local cemeteries searching for my own tombstone. Checked the obituaries as best I could, usually by looking over the shoulders of people reading newspapers. What finally convinced me was returning to my office. I hung around there long enough – and believe me, it was a long time – that someone finally came out with:

"Whatever *did* happen to so-and-so? You know, the tall fair-haired one, always in a sharp suit?"

"Just disappeared. Got sick of his life and vanished – it does happen. Police checked it out and could find, I quote, 'no evidence of foul play'."

My name? Does it really matter?

Katie does. She's just terrific.

She's sitting across the small living room of her small flat right at the moment, doing the crossword in the evening paper. And ... the way she frowns when she's concentrating. The way she taps her pen against her teeth. She never does this when she's in company, is aware there's someone watching. I could watch her all evening, and feel sad at the knowledge that, sometime around eight o' clock, she's going to go out. She's been discussing it on the phone. A friend's birthday party, at a bar in Covent Garden.

If I went with her, I'd have to walk, some half dozen miles. No car or bus or taxicab will carry me along these days. Only the earth supports me. So thank God she has a ground floor flat.

I just woke up one morning and had faded. And it took me almost half a day to realise I wasn't dreaming. I don't even like to think of the screaming panic that overtook me after that.

Two things convince me I am not dead. One, I don't *feel* dead. You should be aware of it, surely?

And second, I can hurt myself. Not with or against any object. I cannot pick up a knife, for instance. I cannot throw myself face-first against a wall, since I merely pass through it. Setting my palm against something very hot does not work either.

But I can bite my own lip till it bleeds. Dig my fingernails into the soft flesh of my arm until I can stand the cumulative pain no more.

No. I'm not a ghost.

What am I?

*

It's one o'clock in the morning now. I'm waiting for her to come back. Not angry or jealous at all. Just really looking forward to it.

She's adorable. I've seen her angry, bored, confused, and extremely happy. Scruffy, naked, getting dressed.

She seems content living alone. She has no boyfriend. She brought someone home from another party, ten days ago, and had sex with him, but it was only that, and she seemed glad when he was gone. Did I watch? Only for the first couple of minutes, before stalking out of the bedroom.

A cab is pulling up outside now. I can hear her voice. And another, deeper one. One with a strange tone I can detect straight away. Is something wrong? I head for the front window.

There are others like me. I run into them, once every so often. And they look no different to the solid people on the street. Except, they'll be standing there, and all of a sudden a pedestrian will walk right through them.

I've tried talking to a few of them, and they are all the same. They seem offended by my noticing them, and bored by my presence. None of them strike me as particularly nice people. Few of the conversations have lasted for long.

Am I like that?

Something's wrong, I'm sure of it. Katie has got out of the cab now, clutching a silver balloon. But the driver has got out with her, mumbling something about 'accompanying her to the front door'. Which taxi drivers almost never do.

I look at him, and see trouble.

He's big and round and unclean. Over six foot tall, almost as wide. And with thick, dishevelled hair. And with a patina to his skin, under the streetlights, which looks filthy compared to Katie's.

Although I have to admit, almost anyone looks grimy compared to my Kate. The constant showers she takes. The creams that she rubs into her pale skin. The *care* she takes of herself. I have never known anything quite like it.

The cabbie keeps trying to touch her shoulder as they walk to the front door. He's talking to her, something about the dog races at Walthamstow. And she, a fixed smile on her face, is pretending to seem interested, God bless her. But she's scared. She's picked up the same vibes that I have, by this time. She's fumbling in her purse for her keys. But the fear has made her uncharacteristically clumsy, and she can't quite seem to get them.

I know perfectly well that I can't help her. But it doesn't stop me trying. I just step out through the front wall of the building, march up into the guy's face and yell out, "Leave her alone, idiot! What makes you think a girl like her would *ever* be interested in a slob like you?"

And of course, he doesn't hear me. You'd think, when I yell that loud, solid people would detect something. A faint vibration. A faint breeze.

They don't though. So much for theory.

"Lived here long, have you?" he's asking her now. "Nice area."

And he's straining at the leash, as though he's been out with her all evening, is now hoping she'll invite him in for coffee.

What is going through his head? Nothing rational, for sure.

Katie reaches the door, finally turns up her keys and, quickly working the lock, lets herself into the lobby, slams the door behind her. Leaving him just standing there.

Well done, girl.

Except the big unkempt man stares at the woodwork for a full minute – I am standing next to him, watching him intently. And then mutters 'bitch'.

I throw a punch at him, and it passes right through.

He turns back to his cab, climbs in. But sits there for another full ten minutes, watching her shadow pass across the now-drawn drapes at her front window. Katie doesn't seem to be aware he's doing that.

Is there any way that I can warn her?

*

I don't know what happened to me. I don't know how it happened.

But – most frustrating of all – I don't know why it happened.

There was nothing special about me at all. Except my parents died – a car crash – before I was old enough to remember them. I was brought up by a much older uncle and aunt. And they were decent enough to me, except there was never really any feeling between us.

I drifted into my career. Drifted into most things. Never married, or moved in with anyone. Just dated the occasional woman for a while, and did the one-night horizontal thing with more than a few. Good looking, well dressed, always.

Had no special friends. I always put that down to jealousy.

And then one morning at the age of thirty four – as I said – I woke up and was still in this world, but no longer a part of it. No one could see me, hear me. And I couldn't touch them. I pass through anything solid, or else it passes through me.

Then how do I eat or drink? I don't. It doesn't bother me. I have to sleep on the ground, and most days I wake up cold and aching. I seem to be ageing, just like any normal person, though. In which case, sleeping in that fashion is going to be real hell a dozen years from now.

Surely, you are saying now, I've got it wrong, I *am* a ghost. Except that ghosts don't hurt, or age.

What am I?

There's a fragment of verse from my childhood that comes to mind when that is asked. I'm not sure if it's a real, written poem, or just a piece of doggerel. But it starts with something like *yesterday, upon the stair* and goes on to talk about a man who wasn't there. I seem to recall it ends with the narrator wishing that he'd go away.

Is that what I am? A man who isn't there?

And is that my deepest, secret wish?

*

The thing with the cabbie worried me a lot, and I stayed up most of that night, watching over Katie. Who was completely unaware of what had happened after she'd come in, and slept like a baby.

It's what I love best, watching her while she sleeps.

Her breathing. The occasional flutter of her long eyelashes. And the perfectly untroubled look on her smooth, heart-shaped face.

Her eyes are closed though.

Let's revise that. What I *really* love best is the moment in the morning when she wakens, and those eyes of hers come open.

She spent an hour in the morning doing her usual things, watching the TV and sipping herbal tea and munching toast. Showered, made herself up in her underwear, then slipped into a nice new suit.

It's a long day after the door bangs shut. Sometimes I go for a walk, but there is not much else to do. Once she forgot to switch the TV off – albeit the sound was not on – and that was terrific. I sat watching it all day. But mostly I just wander round her home admiring how nice she's made it. So stylish and charming, so co-ordinated, and with little pieces of art scattered about.

Around ten o'clock, I hear a clatter from the front door and walk back into the living room, puzzled. Is she back already? Has she forgotten something, or had to abandon work?

There's another slight rattle at the door, but her key doesn't appear to be working in the lock.

The door comes open suddenly.

The cab driver from last night is standing there – I step backwards with shock.

In his right hand is the credit card he's jimmied the lock with. I always thought she ought to change it, get a deadbolt too – how can I tell her that?

He just hangs there for a short while, like a big greasy balloon, his eyes scoping the flat. Doesn't see me, of course. He believes there's no one home.

Comes in, shutting the door very carefully behind him. There's no method to his madness. He's not wearing gloves, has to be leaving fingerprints everywhere.

Does he have a record? I wouldn't doubt it. There's that surly, watchful look to him, as though he's gazing out at the world from beneath a tarpaulin. His teeth are bad. His skin is full of pores. He moves silently enough, but there is nothing delicate at all. Nothing but heavy crudeness.

By the look of him, he smells, but that is something else I've been deprived of. Scent is a matter of tiny particles touching against sensory organs. Particles, however tiny, only pass straight through me.

I haven't reacted in the slightest, apart from stepping back. I'm standing rigid, frozen with shock, and my heart is pounding dreadfully. I consider trying to attack him – but I already did that last night.

I decide to just watch him, find out what he's up to.

He starts looking round the whole apartment, taking his time over it. Arrogant, or just completely crazy? Reaches out every so often, runs his fingertips across an ornament, a flower pot, a little painting.

Then he goes into the bedroom. Sniffs at her pillow like a dog. Then goes over to the chest of drawers. Opens the top one. It's full of her underwear.

He lingers.

And I finally go completely berserk. Howl at him. Try to gouge his face with my nails from behind. Even attempt picking up the bedside lamp and hurling it at him.

You'd think, under circumstances as extreme as this, I would be able to do something, the collective force of my horror and outrage forming itself into something palpable.

You'd think. You can go on thinking till the sun freezes over.

He doesn't take anything. Just stares for a long while. Touches. And then, finally, goes.

I'm doubled over by this time, exhausted and panting from my efforts, shaking all over, my heart trying to burst.

This won't be his last visit, I realise. And there has to be *something* I can do.

If a person can just one day fade, then can't he one day ... unfade?

*

All the rest of this day, I've tried everything that I can think of. Tried imprinting a message in the carpet. Tried moving a pencil on her coffee table by sheer force of will. There is a computer in her bedroom, and shouldn't I – creature out of sci-fi that I have become – be able to do something with that?

And now she's home. And she's completely unaware what's happened. I'm following her from room to room, trying to get in her way, trying to knock things from her hand, shouting, "Katie, you just have to *hear* me! You have to realise the *danger* that you're in!"

She frowned once, but she was only trying to decide whether to use olive or sunflower oil in the salad she was making.

Now it's nine o'clock, and there's a party starting upstairs. People coming in through the lobby, laughing, loud. Music, too much base, a ceaseless thumping. It's just irritating though, not too obtrusive. Katie frowns again, and curls up on the sofa with a book.

I'm practically out of my mind, on the verge of tears. Can't think what else to do.

Only pray that he won't come back. Only pray a look around was all he wanted.

Pray to who? It says nothing in any bible I can think of about someone waking up one day to find he's faded. And so, which god is responsible for me?

*

Eleven. The party is still going on. But Katie is getting ready for bed. That's one of the endearing things about my Katie – she can sleep through anything.

I try writing a message in the steam on the bathroom mirror.

I've yelled myself hoarse, but keep on, though it hurts me.

An almost physical pain surges through me at the precise moment she clicks off her bedside lamp. Is the man waiting outside again? And did he see her window darken?

I'm kneeling on the floor beside her, watching her sleep as never before. Feeling every minute pass. I'll be this way till dawn, if I am lucky.

Midnight. The front door gives a faint rattle. And my hopes are suddenly dropped into a vast, bottomless chasm.

What I've feared all day ... has started.

*

I rush back into the living room. Hurl myself at the man. He just steps forwards – and is behind me.

I whirl back, begin to bellow, *"Katie! Kate! Get out of here!"*

And she has heard something now, though not me. I can hear her sitting up in bed. The light clicks back on.

The man waits, perfectly still, for her. There's no expression on his face to tell what he is thinking.

When she steps into the doorway, she is just wearing her small, short nightshirt. Light washes across one side of her body, but the rest is silhouette.

There's still music coming from upstairs.

She sees the shadowed figure of the man. Jerks. Gasps. Her hand goes to her mouth.

"Scream, Katie! As loud as you can!"

Her eyes go blank and watery. Her voice is very small as she asks, "Who are you? What do you want?"

I attack again. It changes nothing.

He steps up to her, reaches for her shirt. Now, at long last, her mouth begins to open in a piercing wail.

He tries to clamp a palm over it. And she bites him.

He yelps, grimaces, looks offended.

And then punches her square in the face.

And something changes in his eyes. He's forgotten about anything but hitting her, by this time. First with his fists. And then with the grapefruit-sized marble sculpture on the coffee table.

*

Did I just stand there, numbly watching it? Of course not. I cannot recall precisely what I did, what things I yelled out as I did them. But I know they altered nothing.

It is dawn by now. The man is long gone. Katie lies on the floor of her sweet living room, blood drying in her hair. The newborn sunlight from the window touches her cheek, making it almost glow.

I've been in the same position, kneeling over her, for hours now. But that doesn't matter. I'm still sobbing hugely, though the actual tears gave out a while back.

Clutching my forehead. Rubbing my face. Trying to think of some way to make everything all right.

It isn't just that she's gone. Nor the manner of her passing. Isn't simply horror, grief.

I keep ... remembering everything about her. The way she'd lean forward to put her make up on. The way she'd tuck her legs up under her. The way she'd smile, when on her own, at nothing.

Talking on the phone. Sitting naked on the edge of the bathtub, a magazine on her knees.

Sleeping.

Opening her eyes.

My body's being racked with constant shudders, like the aftershocks of an earthquake inside me.

I've never felt anything as terribly as this before, including my own fading.

And that was when it suddenly struck me. A fierce bolt of revelation.

I abruptly knew why I had faded from this world.

It was because I had never properly belonged to it.

The couple who had raised me? My colleagues at the office? The women I'd bedded, and the occasional 'girlfriend' I'd towed around behind me like some small bewildered dog?

I'd never given a damn about them, really. I'd never, my whole life, genuinely cared about anyone sufficient to have them care about me.

Until now.

Until, however much I cared, it made no difference.

Till too late.

Katie was so horribly still. Forever still. I couldn't bear it.

So I asked her, in a fragile whisper, "Please open your eyes?"

*

Later in the day now. I could not stay there forever – no one could – but I have not travelled far. I've wandered out into the lobby, and am now standing – lost in something that doesn't even pass as thought – in front of the staircase. Occasionally, one of the neighbours will go in or come out, unaware of what has happened as yet. And they'll walk towards me, pass right through me, going about their individual business, with their eyes fixed straight ahead.

That old doggerel is running through my mind, by this time. But the words have changed. They now go:

Yesterday, upon the stair,
I saw a girl who was definitely there.
She wasn't there at all today.
I do so wish...

Balancing Act

Jason was playing up this morning. Yesterday it had been Melissa. They took turns regularly like a braced team of interrogators alternating between nice and nasty, and the confession they required was 'I love you'. A test. Jo had never failed it once.

It was November, and drizzling outside the house, so breakfast was a hot one. Scrambled eggs and toast soldiers, and the mugs of drinking chocolate the children insisted on morning, noon and night, not understanding dentists yet, Jo loving them too much to start refusing. The risk of a few fillings, or the memories of cosiness a mug of chocolate invoked – which would be more important in their later lives? Balance was everything, like riding a unicycle with a shopping basket in each hand. Balance was God.

Jason knocked his mug over. Melissa smiled angelically. Jo mopped up the mess and got them ready and packed them onto the school bus.

And, as always, time seemed to shift into a lower gear the moment they were gone. The house became colourless as putty and very quiet. She thought that she could hear the sea. Over the street, a gull screamed.

She made her own breakfast, cold cereal and a cup of coffee, and listened to the radio for a few minutes without hearing what the disc jockey was saying, before angrily slamming it off. Then she began the washing-up.

Christopher phoned at eleven.

"I can't make it again this Sunday." The line from London was so fuzzed she could not make out his tone of voice.

"You bastard," she said.

"Sorry?"

She repeated it.

"Oh. Right. Thank you. Alex has – hang on a minute – " And his voice could be heard away from the mouthpiece, talking to his secretary, laughing. He sounded clearer, right then, than he ever did when talking to Jo. Not the line's fault at all. He came back inside a minute.

"Where was I?"

"Alex."

"Right. He's called a Sunday meeting on the Saunderson account. If we get this – "

"If you get this – "

"I'll be able to send the kids another hundred pounds a month."

"They don't want money, Christopher. They want *you*."

"I think I'll be okay for next month."

"It's not good enough. You *promised*."

He paused a long while. Then he said, "Look, this telephone line is terrible. I think I ought to go."

"*Christopher?*"

"I don't want a row, Jo. Love to the kids. Lots of love. Okay?"

"*Wait*," Jo said. But he was gone.

*

Today was Friday. One full day and a half until Sunday. Jo did some shopping on Pier Street, then walked down to the promenade, string bag swinging loosely in her grasp. Ketchup, alphabet spaghetti, biscuits. A bag of wild rice for herself.

A man walked by with a bedraggled dog. The anglers were out again, rows of dark, hooded backs, immobile against the cold and damp as though they had been painted there. Didn't they have homes to go to?

The sea was the same colour as the sky, which was the same grey as the promenade. Jo felt trapped between them. She increased her pace.

It was lunchtime now. What passed for crowds in this place bustled on the pavement at the far side of the street, seeking the steamed warmth of the cafés. The technical college was at this end of town. The pub was fifty yards from it. Red-shaded lanterns lit the insides, and Jo could see even at this distance that the place was full to bursting.

She hurried across the road and forced her way in past the packed bodies at the door. Michael was in the corner, crammed into a red velvet seat, talking to three older men and women who had to be colleagues of his. He noticed her at once, and waved, and ordered the others to squeeze up further to make room.

They kissed. Quite a few of Michael's students were here in the pub, and so he made a small production number of it.

"I'm not sure I can make it on Sunday," Jo said. There was nowhere to put the shopping bag. She wedged it between her feet.

"Oh?"

"Christopher's not showing up again. He rang this morning."

"Thank. You. Christopher." Michael slumped back as far as he was able, rolled his eyes ceilingwards, sighed. "Cigarette?"

"Thanks."

"You! Block'ead!" Michael called to the nearest male student, a slim blond boy. "Give this lady a cigarette. And while you're about it, give me one too."

The blond boy took his time lighting Jo's, smiling at her all the while.

She nodded her gratitude, inhaled deeply.

"Don't you ever buy your own?" she asked Michael.

"Me? I've given up." He wasn't particularly handsome normally, but his face became beauteous when he grinned. He had been divorced the same length of time as Jo, two years, and had a child of his own somewhere in Essex. His hair was curly as black wool, with a slight balding patch at the crown.

"So," he said, "where do we go from here? Regarding Sunday, I mean."

"My place?"

"Can't you get someone to look after your kids for a few hours?"

Me drop them as well as Christopher? she thought. "It's not fair on them."

"And what about us? Coming round there with your kids hanging about just isn't fair to us."

"How would you know? You've never even been."

He looked away from her when he said, "We're not starting *this* all over again, are we?"

Nobody else was listening. Nobody was watching. Crammed into an alcoholic Black Hole of Calcutta, they were alone as long as they didn't raise their voices.

"Can we go outside?" Jo asked.

"No." He still wouldn't look at her. "If we do go outside we'll have a blazing row and God knows I don't want that. I had it – damn – I had it all planned out. Lunch at *La Cappella's*. A chilly but romantic walk along the cliffs. And then back to my flat for a while. A few pathetic hours."

"Next you're going to say, 'Is that too much to ask?'"

"Right. Spot on. Give the lady a coconut."

"The children aren't going to eat you, you know."

Michael gave a short, humourless laugh. "Don't you believe it."

She looked away herself and stared at a faded patch on the red flock wallpaper by the window. A red-framed notice hung above it. Anyone under eighteen years of age was barred from this place. The pub was unbearably hot after the stiff wind of the promenade. The smell of beer clung about it like tar. A precise layer of cigarette smoke divided the room into upper and lower halves. She exhaled with her lips pursed, adding to it.

"How's your little girl?" she asked the faded patch.

"Gemma? Got the flu, so I hear."

"That's tough. Do you miss her?"

"Yes, of course."

"Sometimes? Always? Occasionally?"

"All the time, I suppose. It's only when I stop moving I really notice it."

"Are you moving now, or standing still?"

"I'm not sure," Michael said.

Jo mashed the cigarette out. "And that's what this is all about, then? Romantic walks? Lunch? Me? A method of propulsion?"

"That's not fair."

"No," Jo said, relenting a little. "No, I suppose it isn't. I'm just quite angry, that's all."

She lowered her head, staring at her shopping, and his hand came up without her seeing it and began to massage the back of her neck. "Look at me?" he asked.

Slowly, she looked.

"Like what you see?"

"Sometimes."

"Give me time," he said. "That's all I'm really asking. Give me a little more time."

"Sunday?" she said quietly, facing him now, challenging him.

He grinned. "A little more time than that."

Outside, just above the promenade railings, Jo watched a flock of gulls mobbing one of their own kind. Screeching, flapping, stabbing, trying to pull the isolated bird a hundred different ways. All over a tiny scrap of fish, as bright as silver.

*

She got home, horrified to find the children standing in the porch. Nothing wrong. Simply that the central heating system at the school had broken down, everyone had been sent home.

They played in the living room all afternoon. The carpet developed an upper layer of clip-together building bricks, plastic animals with moving joints, plastic houses, plastic trees, a scattering of marbles large as golf balls, colourful as dreams.

She had not told them about Christopher's call yet.

Or about Michael. Why not about Michael?

She had not told them anything at all, yet.

*

They were tired now, as exhausted as she was, and while they sat in front of the telly and watched cartoons she went and made their tea. She came back with the loaded tray. The children both looked up at her.

"Daddy phoned this morning," she said, very slowly. "He's not coming again this Sunday."

Going Back

Jason stared back at the television screen. Melissa began to cry. Jason grabbed hold of the remote and turned the sound up.

*

Michael phoned. "Any luck with a babysitter yet?"

She thought of lying. Could not. Not to him. "I haven't tried yet."

"Ah." Michael became very quiet and thoughtful – she could almost hear his brain ticking across the line. Decision time.

Finally, all he said was, "I love you Jo."

"I love you too."

"Try? For me?"

"I'll try."

When he was gone she made a few half-hearted phone calls, all ending in small laughs and apologies and a shaken head which nobody could see and "That's all right, I'm sure I'll find someone," on her part.

*

Saturday was shopping proper, with the kids along. Melissa stopped to watch a woman demonstrating make-up and Jason got bored. Jason stopped to watch a western on a video machine display and now Melissa fidgeted with boredom …

The shopping centre had been built twelve years ago, and at the centre of it was a play area for kids. It had not rained since yesterday afternoon and the apparatus was dry but very cold. Neither of the children seemed to notice. The sea wind whipped around them as they played, yanking their hair into fluttering streams, turning their cheeks red and their eyes to liquid jewels.

And Jo became one of them, immersed amongst them, laughing on the rocking horse, shrieking as she pushed the swings. But all the time watching her children, making sure they didn't hurt themselves, looking out for slippery patches and for strange men in the shopping crowd.

Balance. The see-saw had gone rusty over the years – however hard Jo pushed it never seemed to swing her way.

"Mummy, let's go on the roundabout?" Jason asked.

"You go. Mummy wants a rest."

100

There were benches provided for adults, all but abandoned today. Two old ladies sat and watched the children play and chattered to each other. Jo went to pick up her shopping bags from where she had left them by the side of the swings; straining to their weight and looking up, she saw Michael's head, bald patch and all, bobbing away through the crowds towards the nearest exit. She took a hurried step forward and there was a yell from behind her. Jason had fallen off the roundabout, grazed his knee. His eyes asked, why weren't you looking after me?

Michael phoned again at suppertime.

"I saw you with your kids today."

"At the playground. I know."

"They looked like nice kids. You seemed … very happy."

Jo hesitated at that. She had never considered what she and the children looked like to the outside world before.

"Yes, " she said at last. "Yes, we all were."

"I thought of making my presence known," he said. "But it seemed like I'd be intruding."

Jo thought of Jason with his grazed knee, accusing eyes.

"Look," said Michael, "have you worked anything out for Sunday yet?"

"I tried a few people, but they're all doing things. No chance."

"So lunch is off then?"

He was getting slightly frustrated and angry; she could feel it.

"You could find a sitter if you really wanted to," he said.

"Put them with complete strangers? Yes, I could do that."

He asked quietly, "Don't you have *any* life of your own?"

And she hung up on him.

*

It rained all that night and into Sunday. Jo lay awake listening to the rain pounding like fractured steel against her window. Her last thought was of Michael, lying alone in his own bed. Her last memory was of the digital alarm on the bedside cabinet blinking four o'clock in bright red figures.

In her sleep she dreamt of the gulls. She was one of them, the one with the silver scrap. The others were pulling it this way and that, stretching it, trying to tear it into separate parts to satisfy them all.

It was her love.

The rain eased off around eleven the next morning and the sun slipped palely out. Everything in the gardens back and front glistened beneath a clinging film of water. The windows of the house themselves were streaked and dappled like translucent shells.

The children were quieter than normal. They were still in their pyjamas, Jo was in her dressing gown; they played a gentle game of snap for half an hour before Jo got changed into a rill-neck top and jeans and went into the kitchen to make the lunch.

Perhaps, she thought, he will come.

She laid the table, served the meal. The dining table was at the rear of the front room – it was only when she got up to remove the empty plates she noticed Michael's hatchback parked outside the front, a shadow silhouette through the net curtains.

"Pudding, Mummy?"

She waved her hand for silence without looking back. Walked closer to the curtains. Michael had got out of the car now, was coming down the path. Stiffly. Cautiously. She could not see his eyes, but she could imagine the wariness in them.

His hand lifted, but he did not push the bell.

His arm wavered, then came down. He thrust his hands into his pockets.

Michael.

She envisaged, as soon as he got back into the car, a sudden revving of the engine, then a burst of speed. Gone. Goodbye forever. Free. Instead, the car lurched forwards a couple of yards only and the brake lights came on. He could see her through the curtains and was staring directly at her, waiting for her.

The engine was still running when she got into the passenger seat, closed the door. The heater was on, making a shallow noise in the background.

"I can only stay a moment," she told him.

"The kids. I know."

She looked at him curiously, as though seeing him for the first time. "You almost made it."

"Yeah," he laughed, staring at his hands on the steering wheel. A car taking a short cut flashed past in the opposite direction. Beyond the windscreen, gulls spun like windborne paper scraps against the backdrop of the sky. Everything distant. Everything moving so fast and far away. "So," he said, echoing Friday. "Where do we go from here?"

"That's up to you."

The wind threw dead leaves, like soggy cardboard cut-outs, up against the car.

"I love you," Michael said.

"Don't confuse the issue."

Skin Two

2006: Second Birth

You are staring through two eyeholes at a mirror, in which you can see reflected the silvery mask which has been covering your face the past couple of hours. There are thin cables running from it, all hooked up to monitors. The display panels of which pulse and beat and flicker as though the mask is actually a living thing.

The room is white and brightly lit. A doctor and two nurses are standing in hushed attendance.

Back home, you still own whole bunches of photographs of what your face looked like before the house-fire, back when you were eight years old. A charmingly pretty, healthy girl, with the small, even features and high cheekbones which promise a later blooming into teenage and then adult beauty.

Except you never managed to achieve that thing – the blaze, which started with an electrical fault in your own bedroom and spread quickly to your quilt, snatched it from you.

Plastic surgeons did as much as they could. Not enough, though, to prevent passers-by from flinching when they see you in the street. Or else, even worse, staring. You have little social life and you have never had a boyfriend.

This doctor, however? Steps up till he is beside you now, peering into the mirror himself and gently smiling.

"Almost time."

It has already been explained to you that they have taken a computer-generated image of what you *should* have looked like at your age, and used it as the template for the inside of the mask. There is no exaggeration here, and no deception. Your appearance when the mask comes off? Should be how nature intended you to look at twenty six.

Softly, the doctor begins unclipping all the cables.

"Nervous?" he asks.

Pointless question, and he knows it. You've been shaking for some time now. What if this procedure doesn't work? Though there's one small consolation, if you're cynical about it. Whatever the end result, it could hardly make things worse.

The mask is loose by this time. The doctor moves behind you and undoes the buckles at the back. Then smiles again, over your shoulder.

"Shall I do the honours, or would you like to?"

He seems wholly confident, but it does not osmose to you. This is not simply your only hope, it is your last one.

You have had to be so strong for the past practically two decades, though. Can't you be as strong for just a minute longer?

Surely.

So you say, "I'll do it."

And then raise your trembling fingers to the mask.

You are lost in a great deluge of tears a few seconds later. Never believed – never *believed*! – this was possible at all.

It's a reaction that the doctor seems to be expecting. He waits patiently for your delighted crying to subside, a beam on his face of the 'never doubted it' variety, in spite of the fact that this whole procedure is still in its early infancy. Even hands you a tissue when your sobbing levels out.

You dab extremely tentatively at the fresh synthetic skin around your eyes.

Mumble, "I'm frightened I'll damage it."

You've discussed all of this beforehand, but the doctor's smile doesn't alter. He just, patiently, shakes his head.

"It's like real skin, no more and no less. It breathes like normal skin does, and lets perspiration out. Looks exactly like it, feels like it. Achieves the same temperature as the tissue underneath, and has the same elasticity and tensile strength. The only difference …?"

And his smile actually broadens, as though he has just realised what the bonus is.

"It will never age. It'll remain exactly as it is, from this point on"

You are brushing your fingertips across your brand-new features by this time. Carefully at first, and then with increasing vigour, revelling in the carnal sensation of your newly-recreated flesh.

"I'm not sure how I feel about that," you inform him now.

And the doctor simply shrugs.

"After everything that you've been through, I'd just look on it as a greatly-deserved form of compensation."

2008: Second Glance

"All *over*?" your wife gasps.

You nod.

"All over your *body*? John, have you gone mad?"

"Well I could hardly just do my face and hands, now could I? I'd look pretty stupid at the beach."

Her eyes remain wide open, saucer-like, her eyebrows raised and her face stiff. And then … she actually turns away from you, as though she cannot bear the sight of what you have become.

"Myna!"

"You did this without *consulting* me? Are you *crazy*?"

She looks like she's going to faint, grabs hold of the back of a chair for support.

"I knew you'd be against this. But look! Nothing's really changed!"

That makes her stare at you again. And now, there's anger on her face where before there had been startlement and horror.

"Nothing's *changed*? John, your nose is different! Your brow's different! Yesterday you were a black man, and now you're white! So tell me why?"

"We can afford it. And it can be stripped off again any time I like."

"That's not an answer to my question! WHY?"

You try to remain calm, though that is not how you are feeling.

"I just … wanted to see the world through another person's eyes, that's all."

"Then why not a Chinese man? Or a Pakistani? Why did you choose white?"

Myna steps up closer to you, staring deep into your eyes.

"Are you ashamed of being black, somehow? Have you always been ashamed, without me knowing, of your skin, of your Tobagan heritage? For God's sake, why should that be, John? You're the smartest, the most capable man that I've ever met. Came over here with nothing, built yourself into a massively-successful businessman. You're surrounded by admirers. You're respected universally. In heaven's name, why should you be bothered by the fact that you are *black*?"

Your head drops and you stare at your expensive brogues for a considerable while. When you were first discussing the possibility of this with the consultant on Harley Street, the same question – albeit more politely phrased – was asked of you. Skynth, as it is these days called, has been around for a couple of years, but till now it has only been used on injured or deformed people, and on a few very rich older ladies, those taking the opportunity to lose a decade from their faces. Not for this.

When you look back up at Myna, you keep your tone very even as you finally reply.

"It's not about being ashamed, I swear it. It's – for heaven's sake, woman, you know what the score is. Which country have you been living in? However rich I get, however much I might achieve, there'll always be something not quite right. Not quite accepted. An invisible barrier that I can do nothing to break down. And I just want to see, for once, what life is like on the far side of that barrier. Look at the world a different way, the way a white man sees it. Can you honestly blame me for that?"

She seems to take a while absorbing what you've said. And when she at last does, the anger leaves her face. To be replaced by – even worse – a look of astonishment and almost mockery.

"I think all this, John – " and she waves her arms around to indicate the big Bishop's Avenue house they're standing in, the expensive furniture and ornaments, the four cars parked outside, "has finally gone to your head! You think you can *buy* being *white*? You don't need a skynth-doctor, John. You need a head-doctor."

The fire in her eyes cools down and hardens to contempt. And then she flicks one of her hands at you, dismissively.

"Get away from me now. I'm still waiting for my husband to come home."

You're sick and tired of trying to be reasonable and so, at this, you turn round on your heel and then go slamming out through the front door. Soon are marching down the pavement. Head bowed. Breathing heavily.

She's just confused, you tell yourself. And probably slightly in shock. She'll see your point when she calms down and really thinks about it. Then, she'll come around.

You are under the impression you've been going towards the Heath, but anger has blinded you and you are actually headed quite the other way. You only realise this when you finally reach the roaring, fume-belching dragon that is the A1 urban autoroute. You're not nearly in the mood to turn back yet, but cannot cross this street – there's a high barrier down the central reservation, for one thing. So you look about until you see the opening for an underpass.

You're down the steps and half way along it when the group of four kids appears at the other end. They're dressed gangsta style, in hoods, caps and baggy trousers. And they're walking tightly-packed together, the way that teenagers who are looking for trouble often do.

They're skinny, though. Only one of them is tall. You're just over six foot and well-built, and besides, when you first moved here to London you lived in the roughest part of Hoxton and got quickly used to dealing with potential threats like this. Body language by itself should keep them from bothering you.

It's only when they're almost on you that you remember how you must look to them. A Caucasian man in an expensive suit.

Hands grab at you suddenly and you are flung against a wall. Pinned there. A blade presses against your throat, indenting the skin without actually cutting it.

"Wallet!" a voice hisses in your ear.

All over again, you are now fighting to stay calm.

"I don't carry much cash on me. Just loose change. There's credit cards."

"Nah. Give over yer watch, then."

So you slip it quickly off your wrist. It is a Rolex Oyster but ... plenty more where that came from.

The kid who takes it from you holds it up to admire. "Bling!"

And they've let you go, are turning away, moving off. The knife has disappeared into a pocket. When ... the fist of one of the kids, passing by you, suddenly lashes out, catching you under the nose. Your head snaps back against the wall, and you can feel blood running down your chin now.

The pain hasn't really registered as yet. But you are furious.

"I gave you what you wanted! What the hell did you do that for?" you yell out.

Except that – as often happens when you are very, very angry – you've reverted to your old Tobagan accent. Become painfully aware of that in the next instant. Can still hear your own voice, echoing along the tunnel.

The four faces all turn back towards you, seriously hostile now.

"Whatcher talk like that for, man? You dissin' us?" asks one.

They form a new circle around you. The knife re-appears.

2012: First Refusal

"Send him away, mother. I simply am not doing it."

Ellen Partridge-Browne stared defiantly at her own face in the mirror of her dressing room, finding nothing wrong there. She had a quite *beautiful* face, she had from an early age considered. Delicately-featured, smooth-skinned and fine-boned, with shadowing and colouration in all the right places, all of this framed by golden hair and emphasised by lustrous blue eyes. And she owned the most exquisite dimple at the centre of her chin. Which she held higher now.

There was, so far as she was concerned, absolutely nothing wrong with her at all.

She was in a blue silk ballgown, a Dior one worth several thousand euros. And the first party of her newly-adult life was a mere hour away. It wasn't called 'coming out' any more, but that was what it amounted to.

Her mother crouched down beside her, Dr. Dmitri still hovering in the background.

And … Ellen never found it any less than unsettling, gazing at the pair of them, mother and daughter, in a mirror. There was little at all to separate them, despite a gap of twenty seven years. Her mother? Might as well have been her elder sister. That was the good doctor's work.

"My dear," the older woman cooed, "I understand how you have to be feeling. I once felt it too. But you're a grown-up now, sixteen. Able to drive, and vote, and even join the military reserve. When you were a child, looking like that was reasonably acceptable. But the time has come, at long last, to put aside childish things."

She reached across and pointed to the dimple when she said that, and screwed up her nose.

"It's part of what I am!" Ellen insisted now. "More than that, mother, it's part of what *we* are! Look around the house!" It was a huge, six storey one in Knightsbridge. "Look at all the family portraits! *All* the Partridge-Brownes once had a dimple in their chin!"

Her mother's smooth features took on an expression of weary comprehension.

"Yes, I know they did, my dear. But the fact is, they couldn't help it. If skynth had been around at the time, be assured they'd make use of it. Because the women of the Partridge-Browne line? They are like – why, the best of all bred show-horses, Ellen dear, that is what. And, like show-horses, the most important thing is always to improve the line. Constantly. To weed out imperfection. Don't you see?"

Ellen studied the dimple from various angles. And then actually touched it, which made her mother wince.

"I'm not a horse," she finally asserted. "And it stays."

Her mother threw a tired glance back at Dr. Dmitri, and then shrugged.

"If you insist. But don't say I didn't warn you."

The party was in Chelsea, at the home of Alan Marchmont, one year Ellen's senior and the handsomest boy at her school. Captain of the rugby *and* the cricket teams, and well known to have already bedded several of the girls in Ellen's class. Which didn't stop her fantasising about him – quite the opposite, in fact. She was shaking slightly as she went in through the front door.

"Oh, it's Crater-Face," was the first thing that she heard as her high heels began clicking on the marble flooring of the lobby. "Still sporting that mine-shaft opening, I see."

Standing propped against an ornate pillar, dandling a glass of champagne between her viciously long fingernails, was Caroline Tomlinson-Smith. *Definitely* not one of her friends. A famously bitchy slut who'd opted for her first skynth-job at the age of eleven.

Ellen just ignored her, and walked on into the ballroom.

One of her real friends, Sarah Jane Bradshaw, came rushing over to her almost immediately.

"Ellen, what do you think you're *doing*? I thought your mum was going to get the doctor round?"

Ever since she'd known her, Sarah Jane had had a tiny birthmark on her upper lip, and a funny little crease between her eyebrows whenever she frowned. But both had vanished now.

"It's me. It's staying," Ellen announced. "People will just have to learn to live with it."

She gazed around at all the utterly smooth, blemishless, plastically-perfect faces. And, despite her brave words, felt butterflies beating in her stomach.

Sarah Jane left her alone quickly after that. So did everybody else she tried to talk to. They would listen for a short while, but quite obviously not hear what she was saying. Peer instead at her chin, as though she had grown a beard there. And then find some excuse to walk away from her, when they even bothered with one.

After an hour of this, she was starting to wonder if she'd been completely wrong-headed.

Sarah Jane came over to her again, looking dolefully concerned. She had noticed what was happening, and was trying to help.

"It's the *fashion* – don't you *understand*?" she hissed. "You – "

Then she was cut short. Because Alan Marchmont himself was standing over them. And smiling down at Ellen, in a slightly predatory way.

He guided Ellen over, gently and subtly shepherding her, to an empty corner of the room. And then spent the next twenty minutes with her, asking her questions mostly about herself and smiling when she answered.

Before finally touching her wrist and asking if she'd like to go upstairs.

The butterflies inside her stomach tried to stage a mass break-out at that point.

Her first time! With Alan Marchmont! All her lurid fantasies paled into insignificance at that.

And – more important still – he didn't seem to mind at all about the dimple. In his eyes, it obviously diminished her beauty in no way. He'd accepted her for who she was!

She had heard, from other girls, Alan was wonderful in bed. Slow, considerate, and romantic. So what happened next puzzled and – yes – partially startled her.

He didn't even undress her fully. Pushed up her skirt and removed her underwear. Then pulled her top down a little.

And then? He was on top of her. All over her. Inside her.

It didn't hurt. But only because, probably, it was over and done with so quickly. She was still lying there, bemused, when he disappeared into the en-suite bathroom to dispose of his condom.

He'd re-adjusted his clothing when he came out. Smiled at her out of the corner of his mouth, and murmured, "Thanks, kid," before going back out through the door.

Ellen got up slowly, feeling rather stunned, and put her underwear back on. Then stood there for a long while, trying to understand what had just happened.

When she finally went back downstairs, Alan was at the doorway of the ballroom, in a huddle with four of his closest friends. Their heads were pressed together, they were whispering and laughing. Ellen wondered what about.

Alan raised the index finger of his right hand, put it to the centre of his chin, and pressed it inwards for a moment, creating a dimple.

And then shoved that same finger down his throat and stuck his tongue out, making himself hawk.

The rest of them burst out hysterically. Alan held his palm out flat in their direction.

Still chuckling and wiping at their eyes, they all reached into their jacket pockets. And produced a hundred euro note apiece, which they handed over to him.

Ellen was still crying when she got back home. Her mother was waiting for her in the hallway, and she fell into those rather too-smooth, comforting arms.

"There, there," she could hear her mother saying. "You've made a serious mistake, but it's nothing that cannot be put right."

Ellen saw Dr. Dmitri step out gently from the living room.

"After all," her mother whispered in her ear now, "like a well-bred show horse, you're allowed a first refusal. But no more than that."

2015: Numbers Game

27? 28?

I tilt my head slightly to one side, looking at her.

Or maybe 38? Or even 48 these days?

Or even older than that?

There's no way of telling. All I really know is that she's staring evenly at me.

We are both standing in Sartre's, one of the coolest bars in Soho. Charlie Parker – my demi-namesake – is blaring from the speakers, trying to make himself heard above the babble coming from all these tightly-pressed and wildly-opinionated and fashionably-packaged bodies.

Despite the press of which, we have noticed each other almost straight away. She's medium height, very slender, shapely, in a bright red dress which sets off her long auburn hair. She seems to be in red high heels and has accessorised beautifully. And she appears to be in here on her own. Looking for someone?

Me? I'm just over six foot tall, broad-shouldered, even-featured, sandy-haired. I've always dressed well, Armani jacket and trousers this evening, loafers by Paul Smith, and a thin black cashmere sweater rather than a shirt. So I've never had much trouble finding partners for the night. Except that these days…

29? 39? 49? 59?

I've had a little skynth myself, it's normal. Round the corners of the eyes, and to remove a few small acne scars on my left cheek. But these days, now that the procedure is as quick and easy as Botox used to be and competition between the clinics keeps forcing the prices down …

A woman with a few bob in the bank can have herself completely remade.

A man as well, I'm forced to admit. Is she wondering the same thing about me as I am wondering about her?

What does it actually matter? I ask myself now. (Ask myself every time, in fact). I'm hardly looking to marry her. She could be older than my mother but, looking the way she does right now, what difference does it make?

I just can't help myself, though.

Perhaps ... 33?

She smiles at me and raises her glass. I smile back and nod – and she starts coming over. Here we go.

I'm watching her very closely by now, observing the way she moves. Trying to pick up any tell-tale signs. A slight slowness or an awkwardness perhaps, or maybe even a faint limp. There's none of that at all, which ought to reassure me. Except ... by the elongated musculature of her slender limbs, I'd guess that she's someone who swims a lot. A woman with the right genes who takes good care of herself that way can hit sixty and still prance about like someone half her age.

40, perhaps? I'd settle for forty. Me? I'm thirty one.

She introduces herself. She's called Leonora.

"Interesting name," I smile at her. "I'm Robert. Robert Parker."

So we proceed with the usual flirty small-talk, which I'm good at. All the while we do so, though, the numbers are still running through my head. And I'm still on the look-out for tell-tale signs. Leaning in to smell her breath – trying to catch a touch of staleness – when she's talking. Trying to detect any unusual coolness when I dab my fingertips against her skin.

Nothing. And there is simply no visual way to spot a full skynth-job at all. No joins. No seams. No fastenings.

She doesn't appear to be doing the same as I am, and I've met plenty of women who do. Which means? Either she simply doesn't care. Or else it is ominous.

She's young enough in manner though. And even more stunning close up. So ... what does it even matter? I ask myself for the dozenth time.

Within half an hour, she's complaining that this place is far too noisy for a proper conversation. So I take the cue, invite her back to mine, a short walk away.

I pour us wine, put on an album by a very recent band, The Beenstalks. Chat to her about both them and other modern bands. It's another of the tests that I employ from time to time. A woman in her sixties with a full skynth-job might *look* like a twenty year old supermodel, but her shaky knowledge of new music almost always gives the game away.

Leonora, though, knows all about the Beenstalks, and the Dead Hive, the Grandeeze.

Just before we go through to the bedroom, I duck off into the kitchen and dry-swallow a Viagra-C, the newly-improved variety. I never used to need them, years ago. But the plain fact is, uncertainty is potency's worst enemy. And there is *nothing* but uncertainty these days.

It starts working in a few minutes, which is just as well.

Because when she takes her clothes off, everything about her looks flawless and just perfect. But I can't help wondering – I always do – just what might lie beneath that seamless surface. Heavy, sagging wrinkles? Dense orange-peel cellulite? Thick blue veins just underneath the pale grey skin, and liver spots?

27 or 28, I keep telling myself as I climb into bed with her. She's the genuine article. *Has* to be.

The golden rule is the killer, isn't it? Never ask a woman her age?

We go to it for almost an hour, in a wide variety of positions. She is lively, passionate, adventurous, energetic, and she only starts to flag when I do. When it's over though, when we are lying on our backs …

I realise, as usual, I am listening to her breathing. Trying to detect if she is panting just a touch too heavily. Taking rather too long for the gulps of air to slow?

I look across at her. Her gently-tanned body is now gleaming beautifully with sweat, and she has lain one smooth hand flat across her chest. Feeling her heartbeat?

What does it matter? I ask myself yet again. You have just done the deed with a startlingly gorgeous woman. One so beautiful and good to be around that you could easily fall in love with her. Would have, years ago.

Instead of which, I roll over, turning my back to her. And gaze at the far wall of my room, still wondering.

28? Or 58?

It shouldn't really matter.

But it does.

2025: 100%

You have started to realise, the past couple of years, that you will have to get the whole rest of your body done. You were of the opinion for a long time that the face – this marvellous, miraculous face the doctors recreated for you – was enough, but now the truth is starting to become apparent. It is nineteen years since you removed that silver mask, and the rest of you has begun to lag quite badly behind.

That annoys you slightly. You remember how utterly elated you felt when you first looked in the mirror – how could anything match that? But it's a hard physical fact by this time. Besides, *not* getting the full-job makes you, once again, the odd one out.

You walk home from work along streets thronged with Adonises and Aphrodites. Not a single aged or ugly face in sight. No wrinkled hands. No wattled necks. No crow's feet.

Go in through the gleaming metal maw of Tottenham Court Road tube station. There are gorgeous policemen and women stood with sniffer dogs and contents-scanners just before the barriers. Terrorism is still a big problem, and since a terrorist can easily change his appearance, his race, even his outward gender, there is no way of identifying them by sight alone.

The same with criminals, who are almost never caught these days, except in the actual act. You've read somewhere that many of them alter their face and fingerprints some twenty times a year.

You ride the escalators down into the bustly, echoing depths of the tube system. There is human beauty everywhere you look – it always feels strange to you that you were one of the very first, and people used to look at you suspiciously when you mentioned it.

You don't mention it any more.

It's the same in the packed, smoothly-humming carriage of the train.

No one seems any older than thirty at the very most. Everyone looks as though they belong on the cover of some magazine.

The blond guy standing behind you, though, is breathing rather wheezily. And several of the people who've grabbed seats are sitting there hunched over far more than they ought to be.

When the train pulls in at Goodge Street, a gorgeous redhead pushes past you to get out. Except the effort she makes is a feeble one, and she is moving rather painfully, with tiny, hobbling steps.

The doors slide shut. The train moves off again into the darkened tunnel.

All around you there is loveliness. But on the enclosed air of the tube carriage?

The powdery, sickly aroma of human decay.

Too Good To Be True

I kept on thinking that we met by accident, right up to the end. Now, I realise that she sought me out. Smelling something, maybe. Smelling loneliness, and more.

It had been six months since my wife announced she had found someone else and left me, ending what I'd thought had been eight years of happy marriage. Still, I had my work. Which – since I could get by in several languages – involved a lot of travel.

Rome.

Not the first time I'd been here. But that did nothing to lessen the impact of the city's beauty. Nor temper my excitement at being part of it. I was only here officially for one night, but had already arranged with my boss – back in London – to take the next three days off. And he'd grinned a little sadly, understanding my situation. "Why not? Who knows, you might bump into Audrey Hepburn."

"Or someone who looks like her," I'd countered.

Rome.

I could see it through the office window, all through that day's meeting. It was old and yellowing and broken. But it was like a precious jewel.

We finally wound up around seven o'clock. At which point, three of my Italian counterparts announced that they would take me out for dinner.

I'd already developed, from my last trip here, a faint dislike of middle-aged Roman men. So ... fussy. So obsessed with their own immaculacy. You wanted them to drag their ties off to one side. Or wolf their food down, barely tasting it. Or even let out a belch.

The sky would fall in first.

And, after a while pretending to be interested in their conversation, my attention started wandering off to the other tables.

We were seated outdoors, near the top of the Via Veneto.

Rome. Mid-August. Tourist-smothered. Very hot and, this night, very close.

Outside the café next to ours, two tables had been pushed together. And at it were seated some dozen young women in their late teens, early twenties. Some kind of hen party, or just a girls' night out? I couldn't tell. But their vibrancy, their delight in each other, made me want to kick myself that I was in male company tonight.

And in the other direction, two sleekly-dressed and coiffed women closer to my age were locked in discussion so intimate that their brows were almost touching. One of them looked a bit like Carol.

I fought down the pain of that by drinking some more wine.

By midnight I had drunk enough that I could no longer conceal where my eyes were going. My companions fell a little quiet at that, nudging each other with their gazes. Then, the one opposite me – Giorgio – leaned across and asked, "You like Italian women, Alex?"

I could feel how lopsided my smile was as I nodded.

And he grinned, "If you like, I know a house near here – "

Which was the very *last* thing that I really wanted. We all ended up by bidding each other a polite and firm goodnight.

The lobby was deserted when I got back to my hotel. I rode the lift up in silence. Let myself into my room. Which was like a sauna.

So I switched the cold-air blower – not real air conditioning at all – onto full, and then threw open my window.

A tiny naked woman was staring at me from a placard on top of the room's television set.

I'd already noticed her when I'd checked in. She was advertising the hotel's two in-house adult channels.

So I thought, *why the hell not?*

Peeled off my sticky jacket. Then yanked off my tie and shoes and socks. Unbuttoned my shirt fully. Switched on the TV, being careful to turn the sound off – my window looked out over a ventilation well, with several others.

Punched in my room number using the remote. And then turned out the lights.

I sat down in a chair beside the window, started watching. Almost praying that the movie wasn't going to be one of those tacky, grainy, unappealing Seventies-style numbers.

It wasn't. It was modern, high-production and high-gloss. Like the pages of Playboy come to life, except with men and sweat and tattoos and erections blended in. Lots of romantic settings, lots of kissing, lots of foreplay. They added those when they realised there were couples watching.

I'm not sure how much time passed before a light came on in the window to the right of mine, in the ventilation well. And then, *that* pane came sliding up.

I glanced across a moment, worried that whoever was there could see into my room. But my curtains were mostly drawn. There was no way that my new neighbour could see my TV screen.

I could hear high heels tapping around for a while. Then a toilet being flushed, a faucet being run.

Forgot it.

Returned my attention to the next scene in the movie.

Carol and I had watched one of these things once, and she'd grinned impishly, quite enjoyed it. So ... why had we never watched another, in the subsequent six or seven years?

That had never struck me as odd, until now.

I was still turning it over when a voice called out, "Hi, there."

A woman's voice. Very soft and sultry. With a mild American accent.

My neighbour again. Had she just let someone in? Or was she speaking on the phone?

She tried again. "Hi, there?"

And then, "You in room 464?"

Which was me. Her voice was so close that she had to be right at her window.

I immediately switched the TV off. And felt immediately childish. What did she want?

And what should I do? She knew I was in here, and awake, since she'd have seen the flickering cathode lights.

What was up? What exactly was the problem?

I did up a couple of the buttons on my shirt and then, as calmly as I could, opened my curtains wider.

She was leaning out into the well, her smooth, tanned elbows on the sill. And gazed straight into my eyes the first moment I revealed myself.

And held them.

Her eyes. The richest blue you could imagine, with the thinnest ring of amber round the edges. Her face? Lean and golden and utterly beautiful, topped with piled-up jet black hair.

Her smile...?

An enigma.

I could only see the top half of her. She was wearing a black, spaghetti-strap number, and was leaning forward so her cleavage was revealed. Seemed to have a better figure even than the women in the movie. Almost too good to be true.

But, her smile...?

Was it a mocking one?

Had she seen what I was watching – was she going to protest?

The edges of her smile twitched.

"Why did you do that?" she asked.

I straight away felt uncomfortable at her American way of attacking a subject – to a stranger – without the slightest pre-amble.

Forced myself to reply, "Do what?"

"Switch off the movie you were watching?"

Had she seen? I forced my voice to remain steady as I answered, "Movie?"

"Oh, you know! The adult movie on the hotel channel. The porn movie. Was it good?"

Her smile, warm-seeming, was still firmly in place. Was she baiting me? Would she, any moment now, drop it, and offer me some insult, lecture me on 'objectification'?

What exactly had I done to deserve this?

I just tried to look blank. At which, she gave her eyes a little roll before returning her gaze fully to mine.

"Aw Jeez! Are you trying to tell me that you weren't? At one thirty in the morning with the sound right off? So what exactly *were* you watching that way – CNN?"

I began to feel affronted. I'd been doing nothing illegal or even particularly wrong, and she was invading my privacy.

Seemingly playing games with me. I decided to play back a little.

"Maybe I was wearing headphones?"

She glanced across at her own TV, then clucked her tongue as she looked back. "Huh-uh. No socket on these sets."

"Look, what exactly do you want?"

And she tipped her head to one side, her eyes still on mine, her smile remaining at the exact same dimensions.

"Do you mind if I come over there and take a look myself?"

That was when another thought took hold of me –

She disappeared from her window.

That maybe she wasn't a prude, or a cross feminist, or even just being cruel for her own amusement. That maybe she was a hooker of some kind, returning from work, and seeing the flickering lights. Deducing there was some last money to be made.

Any other explanation?

It would have been ... too good to be –

There came the gentlest rap of knuckles on my door.

And I'd already made up my mind by that time. I had never paid a woman in my life. But the night's heat, the city's beauty, the outdoor table, the murmuring women, the chattering girls. And all alone, single. And her, so physically perfect, right next door...

There's a first time for everything, I suppose.

And so I took a deep breath and opened the door.

*

She came straight in, closing it behind her. Stopped me when I tried to switch the lights back on. Walked straight across to the set, an erotic silhouette in the dimness. Dropped into my seat and put her high heels up on the corner of my bed. Picked up the remote and turned the movie back on.

Her smile became a little broader. She didn't look at me again. Just watched, her face giving away nothing but pleasure. Colours from the screen washed across her. Flesh tones, and the blue of swimming pools.

After a while, I moved over and sat down on the foot of the bed myself. Watching her watching the screen.

She must have felt the mattress shift as I sat, but her eyes didn't make the tiniest flicker towards me.

Yet another idea came. She didn't seem to be a hooker. Maybe she was stoned, or slightly crazy.

The film ended finally. All that washed across her body, now, was a snow-storm of electric black and white.

She finally looked at me, and said, "Not bad."

Then her smile failed slightly. "But a little tame."

Deep inside, I dared myself to ask her, "And what would you call 'not tame'?"

And then heard my own voice – almost from a distance – as I accepted the dare.

Her grin returned to its fullest wattage. "Let me show you."

*

Her name was Ginny. She was three years younger than me. She pulled her short dress off over her head, so that her hair unpiled itself and tumbled down. She was wearing nothing underneath.

She straddled my lap, there on the foot of the bed. Pushed me backwards. Started undoing my shirt, and then the rest.

And, for the whole remainder of the night, I was an explorer, she was my guide. The most thorough of guides. Taking me into every sweet-smelling nook and crevice of her body.

We ended – rather like the movie she'd just watched – with me buried firmly in her from behind. And I asked her, "is that all right?", remembering the one time Carol and I had tried this, and the way I'd had to stop in less than half a minute, it was causing her so much pain.

Ginny pressed her cheek against the mattress, and bared her clenched teeth. And let out a long low grunt in which was contained the word "Harder!"

*

Dawn rose. I had dozed a little but was still exhausted. Had I dreamed it? No. She was still lying beside me, naked, fast asleep.

Would she leave when she woke?

Anything else would be too good –

She woke. Smiled at me. Kissed me. Padded through into the shower.

Called out for me to join her. We made love again there, her hanging onto the rail. It looked flimsy. I was surprised it didn't break.

We dressed, went down to breakfast. Talked, finding out about each other. She'd gone back to college, lived in Santa Barbara. She was studying to be an architect.

We collected together maps and guide books, cameras and small bottles of mineral water. And went out, exploring the sun-enveloped city side by side. Still talking. Laughing a lot.

And had sex three more times that day, her taking the lead each time. Once down a narrow back alley, with stray cats watching us. Once under a bridge down by the river. And the last time in a doorway behind a small, scruffy-looking church.

I was ... what? ... a little flabbergasted by the time we'd finished that one. Felt dazed at my own behaviour.

"Do you suppose God was watching us?" I asked her jokingly as we walked away.

"I'm sure that he enjoyed it," she grinned. "That was quite a show."

By that evening, I was eating again outdoors on the Via Veneto. Except it was perfect this time. A small table, just for two. Ginny sitting across from me, the gold sheen of her skin embellished by the candlelight, her eyes seeming very dark.

I didn't look once at the other tables.

We walked slowly back to the hotel, and re-entered my room.

We were down to our underwear – she was wearing some this time – and I was sitting on the bed, when there came another knock at my door. I just watched surprised as Ginny crossed to open it, seemingly expecting someone.

Tried to cover myself up as two women stepped inside.

Ginny just smirked.

"No need for that. They're friends of mine."

They were identical twins, no older than twenty. No taller than five two, five three. Very slender, very pale, with short, platinum blonde hair.

They didn't smile. But they didn't seem embarrassed either. Their light blue eyes studied me.

Ginny shut the door behind them.

They both started stripping off.

I looked at her startled, almost angry. But her grin remained in place.

"Just this once, why not? Just for tonight. This is my gift to you."

She sounded offended by the thought of my refusal.

She stood there, her back propped against a wall, for almost forty minutes. Simply watching, and enjoying what she saw.

And then she yanked off her bra and joined in.

*

Dawn rose. Again, it hadn't been a dream. The twins had not uttered a single word between them all night, and now they were gone. But I could still smell them, and there was a platinum hair on the pillow between Ginny and myself.

She woke, smiled, showered, but we didn't make love this time. Nor for the rest of the day. I began wondering why, after yesterday's escapades.

It wasn't that she was now cross in any way – I could sense that.

So why?

The tension rose between us until, over dinner, I felt ready to explode.

This time, when I opened the door to my room, she said, "Wait a moment", just as though to prolong things still further, make the unbearable worse.

And disappeared through her own door a minute.

When she re-appeared, she was carrying a large, heavy-looking leather purse.

From which appeared, once we were alone ... ropes, and cords, and cuffs, and straps, and jingling little chains. We attached them to each other.

I had never believed I'd enjoy being hurt by a woman. But the kind of pain she caused me – not like ordinary pain, not like catching your fingers in a door jamb. More like ... stepping out into a sweltering hot day, feeling the heat overwhelm your body. More like ... every inch of your skin becoming uncomfortably tumescent.

I had never believed I could enjoy hurting a woman, and mostly I couldn't. But ... how did she know me better than I knew myself? There was one very small, very discreet way, using just two fingers. I don't think I'd ever even consciously imagined doing it. It must have been something from a dream, forgotten on waking.

When I did it, though – her head tipped right back, her eyes squeezed shut, her brow furrowed deeply. And she let out a gasp which reminded me of...

The very first girl that I ever slept with, as I penetrated her.

Or Carol, coming oh so very softly, on our wedding night.

She grinned once the spasm had passed. Conspiratorially.

By the time that we were undoing ourselves and putting things away, Carol had been relegated to the back rooms of my memory. That had been her last full outing. She'd now been replaced by someone new.

*

Next morning, we breakfasted. Then, eschewing our maps, went for a stroll.

We wound up at the top of the Spanish Steps, drinking in the view.

"Perfect," Ginny announced.

Then she stepped forwards, pecked my cheek, and stepped quickly back again. "That's it, Alex."

"That's ...?" I stared at her bemusedly. "What's it?"

"As in Porky Pig." And she began a comic stutter. "Th-th-th-that's all folks!"

Turned away from me with no more fanfare. Began walking down the steps, putting distance between us.

All I could do, at first, was gawp after her, not believing quite what I had heard, what I was seeing. She'd got quite a way before I found the strength to yell out, "Ginny, *wait!*"

She turned and peered up at me, smiling only mildly now.

"Where are you going? What are you doing?" I yelled at her. "Jesus Christ, I *love* you!"

And, for the first time since we'd met, her beautiful face clouded up with anger. Rage.

She began marching towards me, howling at me as she re-approached.

"You do *not* say that! You *never* say that! A romantic dinner? Fine! A slow walk by the river? Those are scene-setting! They're foreplay! But you do definitely never, *ever*, turn round and say anything like that!"

And then she stopped, looked up over my shoulder.

And she said to someone else, "I'm sorry."

Who was she talking to? I was at the very top of the steps.

I craned around myself – and realised she was staring into empty air.

"I'm so sorry," she repeated. "That just blew the final scene. It can be cut, can't it? It can be edited out?"

And I was starting to believe that she was crazy.

When I began to sense something myself.

Nothing but empty air, behind me? Sure. But beyond it...?

I could feel them suddenly, as surely the sun's warmth beating down on me.

Eyes, fixed intently on the both of us. Huge, unblinking eyes. And nothing human.

Had they been there the whole time? Since I had met her? As we had explored each other, deeper and then deeper still. As we had ... performed.

I could feel their gaze hold steadily on me. And ... who did they belong to?

Who was watching us?

What?

How many of them?

In this so very ancient city, full of monuments to ancient gods, with its history drenched in spectacle and blood and murder ... who could tell what might inhabit or survive here?

And what Ginny had said –

Could they – it – somehow record what it gazed down on, for its later pleasure?

My head began to reel with shock. I couldn't seem to breathe, or think straight.

My vision blurred, and Ginny's shape started to move away from me again. And I tried reaching out to grab hold of her, shake her, get some explanation.

My hand closed on empty air, but kept on moving forwards anyway. Because, by this time, I was falling.

*

When I woke, I was in my own room in a hospital. Very neat, very quiet. Apart from a headache, there seemed to be no pain.

I couldn't seem to move, though, and I began yelling. Nurses came in, awfully gentle, very kind in a sad way. My scratchy Italian didn't include medical terms, so they had to find a doctor who spoke English.

He explained to me, as delicately as he could, that my spinal column had been severed in the fall, at the sixth vertebra. Essentially, I was paralysed from the neck down.

He waited a long while until I had stopped crying. Then he assured me new advances in neurology were being made every day. I knew what that amounted to.

I'd be shipped back to England eventually, he told me. But I wasn't ready to be moved for a few weeks.

Several people here have been extremely friendly to me. One of them's a rather doltish crude man with a mop, Carlo, who comes round every night and tries out his few words of English on me.

It was Friday night, and late. I'd been put in a wheelchair, and was sitting there, just trying to sift the jumble in my head, when he sauntered in.

"Treat for you," he announced.

He switched on the room's TV, and found one of the satellite channels. A porn film was playing.

"Can't do no more, but you can still watch. Good, eh?" he grinned, barely seeming to realise how his words echoed inside of me.

He clicked off the light as he went out.

*

It's one thirty in the morning, another hot Roman night. I am sitting in a chair by a partly-open window. The TV is still on, and its glow flickers across me in a perpetual, warmthless caress.

No light comes on in the window next door. It remains darkened.

Man, You Gotta See This!

See, there's this thing about Jer.

There was a Monet exhibition in our city once. I and Kara – my then girlfriend – trooped through with the rest. Gazed upon the garden scenes and renderings of fog-bound London. Were awed by the way the paintings changed with age and failing eyesight. Loved it. But...

There is something more than love, in art. I found that out right at the end.

The exhibit reached its conclusion, you see, in a big square room which just contained one painting. A triptych, they called it. Three almighty canvases put together to form one.

It was water lilies, of course. Took up an entire wall.

And there were benches in front of it, so I just sat down. And then allowed my mind to fall forward into that weightlessness of pastel colour.

I didn't realise Kara had gone wandering back to see the scenes near Tower Bridge again.

When she tapped my shoulder, asked me if I'd been sitting here all this time, more than half an hour had passed.

I had gone completely elsewhere. I'd been lost. Blissfully so.

And Jer would *never* understand that.

Jerry Mulligrew – almost like the jazz saxophonist – my oldest and closest friend. Thirty four, but looking rather younger. Ponytailed and scrawny. Avoider of honest labour, as, for the most part, was I.

Connoisseur of soft and medium-soft drugs. Lover of heavy metal. Expert puller of the student babes at our local bar – thus proof that earnest eyes, a winning smile and a quick sense of humour compensate for what I'd call weasely looks and dubious dress-sense.

Jer just wasn't into beauty of that kind. It was a concept, he often told me, which had had its day. All of that was misty-eyed stuff, far removed from actual life. We were in the Cyber Age now, and that kind of beauty was old hat.

"And we should replace it with what?" I'd ask him.

"Wonderment, man. Just ... infinite possibilities. There ain't nothin' we can't do."

We both lived on Packwell Street, me in a pokey one-bedroom apartment that had had its rent fixed twenty years ago, Jer a couple of blocks down in the loft room of a long established squat. If you walked past late at night, you could see the glow of his three state-of-the-art home computers through the window, like some Cthulhu Mythos otherworldly glow.

Seeing as he hadn't held down a job since the original George Bush, you might ask how he managed to afford them.

Don't ask.

And ... when Old Man Hubert died, it was rather like that thing Dorothy Parker said when Calvin Coolidge – I *think* it was Calvin Coolidge – did the same. 'How can they tell?'

No one could remember when they had last seen him. He'd had his groceries delivered, and he'd never ventured out. He was almost like a mythic figure to most people on the street. He'd lived in the big house at the very end of Packwell, where the street met the hill, rose for a few blocks, and then gave way to shabby-looking woods. Huge house. Old house. Cupolas and stuff. It was surrounded by an iron fence, and all the drapes were permanently closed.

What did he do there?

"He's supposed to be a painter," Ray the Bartender informed us one time.

"No shit? He has opening nights and stuff?"

Ray shrugged. "Never heard of any. Never seen anything by him. S'far as I know, he never even tries to sell his paintings. The word is he's got inherited money."

I exchanged glances with Jer, but he just shook his head.

"No way, dude," he said once Ray had moved off. "I'm not into that art-stuff, but I respect all creators. In a way, I'm one myself. He's old anyhow. We'll leave it till he's dead."

And now he was.

One day, a hearse simply appeared at the end of the road, but with no limousines following it. A coffin was brought out, and loaded in, and then driven away. The front door was padlocked and the windows boarded up. No moving truck appeared.

When I saw Jer that afternoon, his thumbs were pricking, like the witches in Macbeth. He was all keyed up. Then he looked down at my ankle, remembered that I'd twisted it last night – on a loose paving-slab, extremely drunk; he'd had to help me stagger home. And groaned.

"Ah, what the hell?" he philosophised. "It'll probably be months before some lawyer gets around to having the place emptied. We can be in and out as much as we like, take a little at a time. Like – shoplifting, you know? There must be God-knows-what in there."

He was off towards the house alone an hour after darkness fell. Sitting in front of my TV, feeling pretty sorry for myself, I could imagine him prying back the boards.

An hour and a *half* after darkness fell, my phone went. It was Jer, on the cellphone he had bought from Ray a month back.

"Man, you gotta get up here!"

"What are you talking about, bro?"

"Man, you gotta *see* this!"

I felt myself go slightly red. "I'm a cripple, for chrissake! I can't go doing B-and-E in my condition!"

"You get up here right now, man, or you'll forever kick yourself. I shit you not even slightly. This has to be seen to be believed."

What did? I next asked him.

But he told me that he could not even describe it. He gave me details of how to get in.

I was cursing as I limped up the gradient. Two things, apart from the discomfort, really bothered me. Firstly, Jerry often took some kind of upper before heading out on such a venture, to heighten his senses and make his reactions quick. I wondered if his wild excitement was simply the product of some chemical, and nothing more.

Secondly – and this one, honestly, had been nagging away at the back of my mind ever since that talk with Ray ... if Old Man Hubert had been a painter, then what was he painting with the drapes all drawn?

The door might be padlocked, but the metal gates had been left open – forgotten about, presumably, when the hearse had driven out through them. I went down the shadiest side of the house, brushing past a row of trees, and there was the small side window, just as Jer had described, with two thirds of the boards pulled away. There was an overturned bucket to heft myself up from, otherwise I don't think I'd have made it. But my ankle was still hurting like hell by the time I was inside.

"Jer?" I whispered.

A small flashlight came on.

I couldn't see Jerry behind it, but could hear the tremolo in his voice.

"C'mon man! Follow me! You gotta see this stuff!"

He sounded like a little kid who'd just found a dead squirrel.

I hobbled along behind him, painfully aware that if Five-O showed up now I didn't have a chance of running. And I prayed that there weren't any stairs involved.

There weren't.

We went down a corridor into the pitch-black centre of the house. Through a door, which Jer told me to close.

Once I did, a switch clicked – and I was temporarily blinded.

"Jesus!" I swore quietly. "You could have warned me."

"Power's still on. Everything's still on. Seems like most people don't even know Old Hubert's dead."

Or was even alive, I realised.

"So, what's this boundless treasure trove you're so eager to show me?"

I was aware, by now, of the heavy smell of oil paint in the large, windowless room. And there was an easel propped against the far wall. Different colours spattering the floor. This was where the man had worked.

"That's the crazy thing, dude," Jerry now informed me. "All the rest of the stuff in this place? It's in the plastic-dolphin, souvenir-of-Seaworld category. And this old cat had *money*? But the stuff in here ..."

Framed canvases were stacked, facing inwards, thirty or forty deep, against the two side walls. Pile after pile of them. They were ranked according to size. None of them as big as the Monet triptych, but there were some very large ones. There were also dozens as small as an edition of Hustler.

More than a thousand in all, I took a quick guess. The smell of oil paint had grown so strong, now, it was starting to make my head reel.

Why might Hubert paint all these, simply to keep them here and face them inwards?

But then, why would Van Gogh want to go and cut off his own ear?

"Jer," I said to my friend. "I thought you weren't into paintings."

"Usually no, but – "

"Are they valuable?" I cut in.

"I'd suppose so, dude. I can't imagine anybody not wanting to buy them. Take a look."

And he turned one of the largest ones to face me.

*

The truly weird thing was, when I'd gone into that blank at the Monet exhibit, I'd at least still been aware what I was looking at. A pond. And lilies.

But I have simply no idea, to this day, what was actually depicted on the canvas that Jer showed me. Except that I'm sure it wasn't abstract.

A pastoral scene? A garden? A house? Cityscape? Night sky?

I just don't know.

What were the main colours used?

So far as I can remember, *all* of them.

Jerry shook me rather annoyed.

"Hey, man!"

"Wh – "

I looked away, with difficulty.

"Dave? I've been talking to ya, like, the last five minutes. You been dropping too many painkillers?"

I looked back at the painting.

Jerry shook me rather annoyed.

I didn't even say 'wh–' this time. Didn't look around. He had to physically put a hand to my face, turn it.

"Dude, what are you *on* tonight?"

I shook my head, trying to clear it. "Nothing," I replied, trying to hide my own confusion.

Something in me screamed out not to look back at the painting.

"Ain't it great?" Jer was enthusing by this time, though. "And they're all like this, all the ones I've looked at, anyhow. And I don't normally dig this kind of stuff, but these are ... such amazing use of colour! Hubert was a *genius*!"

He set the painting back in place, face inwards. I felt a massive sense of relief.

Now, however, Jerry switched into full Scheming Mode.

"We can't just move them all at once." His tone had become staccato. "What I say is this. We take a half dozen of the smallest ones – "

"*You* take them. I'm a cripple."

"And we show them around some galleries and stuff, and get some valuations. Man, the ones I've seen aren't even signed. I could say that I did them myself."

Which made me wonder if the art world was quite ready for someone like Jerry Mulligrew.

"And if it turns out they're worth something, yeah? We can borrow Ray's pickup and load it up. We might be sitting on a goldmine here, bro!"

He chose five, in the end, of the little ones he liked the best. Helped me through the window, but then let me limp back home myself.

What had happened back there? Just what had I seen? Colours flashed behind my eyelids, every time I blinked.

There was two-thirds of a bottle of generic vodka waiting for me when I got indoors. I finished the lot during the next couple of hours. Don't remember going to bed.

It was noon the next day when I awoke. I was woken by the phone.

*

"Dude?"

My tongue just about managed, "Hi, Jer."

"You've gotta get over here!"

"The house again?"

"No, man. April's!"

April was a waitress he'd been dating – if you could call what Jer did that – for the past couple of weeks. She lived a couple of blocks crosstown, on Miller Drive.

"What's up?"

"I'm, like, scared man. She is really out of it. I think she's gone and done some bad stuff."

"Call an ambulance, then."

"Man, get your *butt* here!"

The hangover drew attention from the pain in my ankle, at least. I went up the short flight of steps to the front door of April's tiny but incredibly neat dwelling. Went to press the buzzer, but the door was off its latch.

I found them both in the elevator-sized living room, April sat cross-legged, and Jer hunkered over her, every contour of his body a map of concern.

Her pretty, fine-boned face was entirely slack. A trail of saliva depended from her painted lower lip into her lap. A pool was forming.

She didn't seem to blink at all. Her pale blue eyes – were they reflecting something?

"She was like this when I found her," Jerry said, his face screwed up with inner pain.

And it was a familiar one. People like us, with acquaintances like ours? Once every so often, a pal, a girlfriend winds up in this state and finishes up in ER. Quite *literally* finishes, from time to time.

He'd just never believed it would happen to someone like April. Yes, she did a little blow, like any normal person. But nothing else that either of us knew about.

She was facing something that was propped against her armchair. I couldn't see it from this angle.

"Tell me what happened?" I asked.

"Man, I dropped around to see her last night, after ... you know! We smoked some, then fooled around a little. I even brought her a gift. Came back here 'bout ten this morning, and she was like this. Her *skin's* cold, man, like she's been sitting here all night!"

There were no spoons, candles, or tin foil near her. I inspected her arms, found no tracks.

Then I looked at what she was looking at.

Jerry ... shook me.

"Dude, what the hell are you doing?"

I had to force myself to look away.

"That's the gift?"

"I thought, why not? We've got plenty of them to spare."

"Jer, there's something wrong with these paintings."

"Say what?" And, incredulous, he almost laughed. "Man, they're just so great. They're ... beautiful. See? I said it. I acknowledged the existence of your kind of beauty."

"Jer, they – "

"It's gotta be some pills or something," he was babbling away, though. "Pharmaceutical smack or something. Man, if I get my hands on whoever gave her *that* stuff – "

And he would not be told otherwise. He took her in a cab to the local ER in the end, bumming ten off me towards the fare.

I followed them out, refusing to glance back.

*

April was in a coma, though the people at the hospital could not discover why. It was not drugs. I went to see her the next day. Swore I could see flecks of surplus colour in her open, staring eyes.

The thing that keeps people like Jer going and makes survivors of them – it is their ability to just move on. It's not that he didn't care. Far from it. It's just that he realised, without having to vocalise it, that continued existence depends on – do I really have to use that old 'moving shark' metaphor?

Over the next couple of days, he hauled the five paintings – he'd taken April's back – around some dozen galleries.

"What is with it with these fools?" he now complained. "They're supposed to be businessmen, and all they do is gawk? I couldn't get a price-tag out of one of them! And for such beautiful paintings!"

And I finally realised what this was. It was all to do with – immunity. Resistance levels.

A disease goes around, see? A plague. And most people succumb. But a few just have something natural in them that subdues the sickness, makes it less effective.

So it was with Jer. He'd always been aloof towards fine paintings. Totally immune to artistic beauty. And so, when the bug had struck, it had affected him to a degree – but had not felled him completely like the rest of us, apparently.

"Jer – " I tried to tell him for the dozenth time.

But he still wasn't prepared to listen. Maybe that was a part of the paintings' limited effect on him.

When he went home, he looked annoyed enough to do something exceptionally stupid.

Which bothered me enough to go around at ten o'clock and check up on him.

*

The door wasn't locked. The pungent aroma of California Gold hit me as I went into the hallway.

There were no lights on in Jer's living room. Just the glow of those three screens. That was strong enough to pick out, on the little dining table, an open jar of pharmaceutical coke and a half-empty bottle of bourbon.

Jer was hunkered over the screen of the middle computer, and there was a scanner humming beside him, and several wooden picture frames lay scattered on the floor.

His back was in the way, so I could only see the edges of the image on his screen. It was enough.

It didn't mesmerise me, this time. Maybe you needed the whole picture for that.

"Jer, what are you doing?" I asked.

When he turned towards me, I could see how out of it he was. His face like a plastic mask in the weird light. His pupils too large, his thin lips twitching. He tried to smile, but it came out as something else entirely.

"They're so beautiful, dude," he informed me, like a stuck record. "Beauty like I've never seen in my entire life. If those asses at the galleries won't show them – well, the whole world ought to see them. That's what art's about, right? It belongs to everyone. The entire world."

His e-mail page was now up on the screen. He turned back to it, and started making attachments.

What the –?

"Jer, no!"

And I started lunging forwards.

He had clicked on 'Send' before my hand could reach him. I stopped, feeling a lot more than helpless, letting my arms drop down to my sides.

"The whole world, man," Jer was mumbling to himself again. "The entire teemin' world."

*

It is two days later, by this time. And everything has changed.

No planes pass overhead any longer. There are far fewer cars, no trains. The mail hasn't come. The mart down the road is running at half staff, and running out of supplies. There are hardly any trucks at all.

Not everyone has a computer, of course. Most of those people are just wandering around, trying to figure what the hell is going on.

Sooner or later, most of *them* go into a loved one's place of work, or an offspring's bedroom. And they do not re-emerge.

This morning, a fire started up near the centre of town. And is still spreading. I can see the vast plume of smoke from my window. And I keep on wondering. Those people in front of their screens down there – do they even move when the flames start to consume them? Chill thought.

The power hasn't gone out yet. Emergency measures, I suppose. I wish it would. Although that might change nothing. It took only the space of one night to put April in a coma. And it's now been forty or so hours for most people.

I ought to go see if she's come around, but cannot bring myself, since I suspect the worst.

Jer dropped round about an hour back. He still doesn't seem to realise what's going on.

As I said, maybe that's a side-effect of his partially-immune reaction to the paintings.

He told me six more times how very beautiful they were.

There's looting.

I keep thinking of places that I've only ever seen on the TV. Craggy places. Dusty places. Places where there is not so much as an electrical wire, but people live there.

They don't even know it, but they've just inherited the earth. Does an absence of technology make one meek in any sense?

Someone just got shot, down at the corner. Is the fire heading this way? God, I wish the power would go out, even though that idea rather frightens me.

Maybe I should try to get away from here, though how or where I simply do not know.

Maybe – better, easier – I'll just go back to the old house, back to that paint-redolent room. Turn one of the canvases around.

And get lost.

The same way everything is lost now.

Beautiful!

Alsiso

In the morning, Beth would paint. She liked the light at that time of the day, the way it was reflected in from the Caribbean. Harriet? She would sleep late, or sunbathe, or swim, or read – often a combination of all four activities. Did sleeping late count as an activity? She wasn't sure.

At lunchtime they would go to La Cocina, a restaurant owned by a local who had lived in San Diego for ten years and spoke good English.

And the afternoon? Originally, they had spent it on Alsiso's little crescent-shaped beach of white sand. That had been before they had discovered the rocks and the caves at the far southern end. No one else ever went there, and after the first couple of months they decided it belonged to them.

Harriet had never known her skin this dark. It didn't look at all like skin to her these days. It looked like oil.

In the early evening they would go back to the simply-furnished apartment they were renting and make love, and this was, without a doubt, the best part of Harriet's day. It seemed incredible to her, now, that she had spent an entire nine years married to Mike and she had never once, in all that time, attained a climax. Sex back then had amounted to lying back and being jiggled for a while. Sex now? She had always imagined – pre-Beth – that it was all to do with mouths. And there was some of that, but it soon turned out fingers were more important.

And it was not even that, she finally discovered. Beth could make her come by simply playing with her nipples for a good long while. At first, that hadn't been the case. In the first couple of months, doing anything short of clitoral, the slowly-shuddering ceiling of the bedroom back in London would come floating back into her vision, and she would go rather numb. But after a while, she had forgotten all that, relaxed, released herself.

Later in the evening? They would hang about the promenade for a while, trying to sell whatever Beth had painted. Alsiso didn't get anything like the number of tourists who visited Cancun, further along the coast. But it got its share, mostly older North Americans.

And then, with money in their pockets, they would head back to La Cocina for their evening meal. They liked the place. It had a courtyard with two lemon trees. The air was fragranced by them. They could look up at the bright, sharp stars. Rodrigo, who owned the restaurant, understood that they didn't eat meat and – unlike most Mexicans – respected that.

This whole business had struck Harriet as odd initially. She had laughed at countless jokes about vegetarian lesbians during suburban London dinner parties ... and now? She *was* one. How had that come to be the case? She had originally thought there was a historical symbolism to the whole 'no meat' thing. Men had traditionally brought home meat – eschewing it proclaimed an independence from them. Now she understood that it was, rather, an attempt to live your life without everyday – and thus unremarked upon – cruelty.

Later, they would prop themselves up at La Cocina's well-stocked bar, start on the tequila and get – usually – rather drunk.

This was how every day had gone for months now. It was good to stop in one place for a while. After fleeing London – they had met at an arts class sponsored by the local council, Beth had been in England as a nanny for six months – they had flown to Seattle, and then made their way down the Pacific coast until Harriet's visa had run out. Now? Mexico. And after Mexico? She had no idea. No plans.

Apart from the early evenings, it was the rocks she loved the best. There was just one flat smooth area on which they could lie naked. Beside that there was a pool perhaps twelve feet deep, half-filled with weed amongst which there lived starfish, hermit crabs, and various tiny blennies. The rest was sharp crags and projections, and was honeycombed with – not caves really – pumice-like tubes, almost all of them leading downwards. Water rushed through most of them, occasionally surging up so hard that it erupted from an opening, drenching them in cool, fine spray. The sounds it made. It was like listening to the ocean breathing.

It would be nice to dive into the water from the rocks, but the sea was rough around here, and occasionally the tip of a black fin would appear for a couple of seconds, something you never saw from the beach. Their apartment complex had a swimming pool, and they confined themselves to that.

Harriet would stare at Beth for hours sometimes, while the woman slept. Beth was so much more beautiful than her. Naturally slim, naturally athletic, small and very blond. She had the laziest, easiest of smiles, even in repose. She refused point blank to divulge her true age – even going to the extent of hiding her passport – but was obviously in her mid-to-late twenties.

Harriet was thirty two. Had never had children – couldn't, something Mike had never forgiven her or let her forget. She had been rather flabby when she had met Beth, but that had now melted away. Why? Simply because she was happier? She had red hair, and was quite tall. She didn't *mind* not having kids, could recall hours spent in the company of recent mothers thinking 'don't you have anything else to talk about, a life of your own, you silly cow?'

Except that, before Beth, she'd had no real life of her own either.

She wished she could paint well enough to make a living. Wished she could do something. Perhaps she should get a job? But lying out here on the rocks, she was entirely happy.

The young man started working at La Cocina in early May. When they first saw him, over lunch, he was sweeping out a corner of the courtyard.

He was perhaps six foot two. Well-muscled, not an ounce of spare fat on him. Wore a white singlet and faded Levis. Had his hair woven into beaded dreadlocks. There were several gold rings on his fingers, and a thick chain of the same around his neck.

When he saw them, he grinned – his face was extremely smooth and handsome. He put down his broom and then came sauntering across and leaned on their table.

"Can I get you ladies anything?" He was North American, they realised now. "Freshen up your water, perhaps?"

There was a twinkle in his eye as his gaze flickered between them, and Harriet realised she was warming to that. She was about to answer, when she heard Rodrigo shouting from the kitchen doorway.

The young man glanced over his shoulder, looked back at them and shrugged, then wandered across to see what the Mexican wanted. There was a hurried, muffled conversation between them, which Harriet could guess the sense of. 'Stop bothering them, dummy – they're a pair of dykes'.

And then Rodrigo sent the young man off into the kitchen on some errand.

"I am sorry about that," he explained when he came over to greet them. "He is new here."

"He being?"

"His name's Cody. Just some kind of drifter. I offered him the spare room at the back and minimal pay to do some odd jobs 'round the place."

Beth looked slowly round the courtyard. "You're not exactly busy here."

Rodrigo grinned, slightly embarrassed. "I know. I've just got a soft spot for strays, I guess." He glanced at their table next. "Can I fetch you more salad?"

Down on the rocks that afternoon, Harriet found herself thinking about Cody. The casual way he had leant on their table. The casual effortlessness of his every move. She liked that. In all the time that she had been with Beth – almost a year now – she had never found herself attracted to another man. Most of them reminded her of Mike, all stiffness and tough outer shell. But there were earlier memories than Mike. For two whole months at university, she had been with a young man not unlike Cody at all – she'd never even told her parents about that. And their lovemaking had been ... *more* than just a ceiling jiggling.

More than even with Beth? She was not quite sure, it was so long ago.

She found herself staring for ages at the blue-white sky though, imagining things.

After a long while, she realised Beth had come awake. She turned her head to see those green eyes staring at her oddly. As though Beth could read her thoughts.

"What's up?"

"It's okay," Beth told her, rather coolly. "I'm not Mike, you know. I'm not about to go berserk because some hunk catches your interest."

"That's – "

"Really? I could see the way you were at lunch. Don't worry about it. I'm cool."

That evening when they made love, Harriet mostly did for Beth, working diligently, deeply, as though in an effort to make up for what she had been thinking.

Cody wasn't there when they returned to La Cocina.

"He only works here days," Rodrigo told them. "I think he went off with some Danish chick that was here earlier."

The next morning was like any other. Sleeping late, sunbathing, swimming, reading while Beth painted. Beth could not afford to work on canvas, used hardboard which she had to prime herself. Her paintings still sold anyway – all of them, eventually.

Cody was up a ladder when they walked into the restaurant's courtyard, replacing some of the red tiles on the roof. He had his shirt off and was sweaty. When he realised they were there, he looked down at them and grinned. "Afternoon, ladies."

Harriet answered him back. Beth didn't.

Down on the rocks all that afternoon, Harriet had precisely the feeling of enduring a long, sleepless night, despite the fact that it was daylight. She felt simultaneously restless and unable to move. Kept closing her eyes and thinking about Cody. Why was the man affecting her so? It wasn't just the memory of the lover at college, it was …

No, damn it! She tried to force that out of her mind.

Cody himself just wouldn't leave her imagination, though. She kept picturing him looming over her, touching her, his bare skin damp and salty. After an age she fell into a half doze, and it was a while before she realised that her left hand had actually moved down between her legs, her fingers were –

"Oh, fuck you!"

Beth's voice brought her awake with a start. She snatched her hand back now, uncertain where to put it.

Beth was up on her elbows and staring at her fiercely.

"I'm right here! Right beside you! Oh, *fuck* you!"

And in the next moment she had stood upright. In the next after that, she took three steps towards the edge of the rocks, and then dived into the churning sea below.

Harriet sat up with a yelp. "Beth, no!"

There was nothing she could do though. The blond head was already moving outwards, appearing and then disappearing behind the tall waves. Harriet drew her knees up to her chest and shivered, frightenedly scanning the surface for any signs of a black fin.

It was five minutes before Beth re-emerged. She was dripping and looked rather cold, but didn't seem any less angry.

"Right next to you," she muttered, snatching up a towel. "And you're getting off thinking about some guy you barely know."

"I'm sorry." Harriet could hear how her own voice had taken on a childish quaver. "I was asleep. I didn't realise – "

They didn't make love that evening, and had their meal at some other establishment than La Cocina. Beth went straight to bed when they got home, and immediately fell asleep, the way she always did when something was upsetting her. Harriet lay awake for hours. She was staring at the darkened ceiling now – had she spent her whole life gazing upwards? And those bad, those stupid thoughts of this afternoon kept flowing through her head.

It was ridiculous. No, worse than that, it was self-destructive and absurd. The time she'd spent with Beth had been the happiest, the most relaxed, most joyous in her entire life. She dearly loved the woman.

And yet … *crazy!*

And yet …

There had always been – she was forced to admit it now – a small voice nagging from a darkened section of her mind. 'Things shouldn't be like this'. She had been brought up from the earliest age to believe woman should be with, marry, men and anything else was wrong. And that was utter, ignorant, out-dated rubbish – her forebrain more than understood that. Yet it didn't stop the little voice. She just ignored it, mostly.

Now, though? Now, for the first time in practically a year, the question had posed itself. Did it have to be this way forever? Mike could just have been a sour aberration. Could she actually find what she needed with a man?

She looked across at Beth, so beautiful asleep. Felt guilty even entertaining thoughts like these. But she simply couldn't help it. It was part of what she was.

Beth was in no better mood by the next morning. Started on a new painting, then knocked it off its easel.

"Shit, I need a break from this. I'm going for a walk. Alone."

She hadn't returned by midday. Harriet thought of going to look for her, then realised how pointless that would be. Behind the modern shoreline frontages, Alsiso was an old and fairly complex town.

A feeling of utter sadness had descended on her by this time, because she'd realised, by now, what she was going to do. Why didn't Beth just come back and stop her, save her, make the thing impossible? Maybe that was why she'd disappeared. Was this some kind of test?

By one o'clock her stomach was growling, the pangs of necessity adding their weight to the whole process. Harriet felt like some lamb leading itself to the slaughter as she made her way to La Cocina. Why was she doing this at all – had she gone insane?

All such thoughts fled from her mind when she walked into the courtyard, though. There was Cody, replacing a broken flagstone. Again, minus shirt.

She ordered some fried eggplant from Rodrigo. Gazed, as she ate it, at the young man's back until he noticed and came over to her. He leaned on her table, as before. His every movement casual, effortless. As before.

Grinned.

"Well, hi there."

"Hello."

"Where's your friend?"

"I don't know. I mean, she's gone for a walk. She's an artist and gets moody sometimes."

"Best to let her be, then."

"Yes." She thought of what to say next. "You look like you're working hard."

"Not really."

"I hope Rodrigo's paying you enough."

A shrug. "I don't need much."

"So then, what do you think of things here in Alsiso?"

"Beautiful views," he replied, his gaze not moving from her face. And here the moment was.

"I understand you have a room at the back. Do you think I might see it?"

And she laid her right hand gently on his wrist at the same time.

There were several crates of tinned chopped tomatoes piled up in one corner, and the bed was of the folding, metal-framed kind with old blankets on it.

"There's even a little washroom with its own shower," Cody told her, nodding to another doorway.

She didn't know what to say to that, so she reached down and pulled off her dress. She'd put on no underwear before she'd come here.

Cody looked her up and down and his grin became broader. "Nice."

She moved up to him, began trying to unbutton his fly, but he took hold of her hands gently and moved them up around his waist.

"Leave Mr. C. alone a while. I'm more considerate that way."

He slipped off his golden rings and chain. And the next thing she was lying on the bed and his head was moving downwards.

His tongue felt slightly rougher than Beth's, but moved strongly, almost urgently. Harriet was just beginning to enjoy it, when she had the most awful suspicion.

Somebody was watching them. She felt entirely certain of that fact.

Her eyelids sprang open, went straight to the front door, which was closed. Went next to the window. It was open. She could make out a palm tree and some thin white clouds high up beyond it. Nothing more than that, though. Nobody there. No face.

The feeling wouldn't go away, though, however hard she tried to ignore it. It made her stiff, and drained all passion from her. In the end, she was forced to pretend that something had happened, the same way she used to with Mike.

Cody got himself up higher on the bed and pushed his jeans down. She felt that once-familiar thrill from college days as Mr. C. bounced into view, alive-seeming and eager. And she wanted to touch it, play with it a while. But Cody was too excited by this time, too driven, impatient.

She bit her lip as he entered her. Then, after a few strokes, started to respond, thrusting back.

The feeling of being watched returned stronger than ever, making her go still again and sapping every last ounce of her pleasure.

In the end … in the end …

She wound up watching the ceiling jiggle for a while.

Cody rolled off her as soon as he was done and disappeared into the washroom to dispose of his rubber. She could hear water running. When he came back in, he flopped down on the bed, ran a hand across her breasts and gave a huge smile.

"You're so cute. And your girlfriend's even cuter. Reckon she'd be interested in joining in some time?"

When she started to get angry, he just looked bemused.

"What problem? We're all freaks when it comes down to it. You should know that better than anyone."

*

She was almost crying tears of rage, mostly directed at herself, as she headed back to the apartment. There, she'd done it! Gone and done it, really, truly! Proved herself 'normal'. And just how had she managed that?

Not only by betraying Beth, but by betraying her cheaply, pointlessly, and joylessly with somebody who couldn't hold a candle to the woman. There! Well done! Congratulations! Did she get a merit badge?

There *were* tears dribbling down her face by now. Not least because she realised she now faced one last decision. Whether she was going to confess all this or not. She couldn't think straight, so she didn't know.

Beth was still out when she let herself back into the apartment. That was very odd. Where could she have disappeared to for so long?

Harriet went to take a shower, and stayed in there for a considerable while, remaining under the jets long after the hot water from the solar-heated tank had run out. She felt no cleaner by the time that she emerged, however. She towelled herself off.

Beth was *still* not home. And it was by now well past three o'clock. The woman had been gone for hours.

*

At nine, a wan, sad shadow of herself, she wandered down to a café on the beachfront, ordered a plate of *refritos* and rice, and barely touched it. Watched the sunset bleakly.

It was dark by the time that she got back. Beth still had not returned. When she let herself in this time, she did not switch on any of the lights. Just sat down in an armchair in the living room and pulled her legs up to her chest. And, resting her head on her knees, accepted the inevitable. Beth knew. Beth had seen or found out. And had gone away.

How could she have done this? How could she have been so incredibly stupid?

She was on the verge of tears again when a car pulled up outside the window, its headlamps sweeping briefly across her. Half a minute later, a key turned in the lock.

Beth stepped in.

Harriet noticed something odd about her right away. She was smiling, but it was not the usual lazy, easy smile that she had become accustomed to. It was a tight thing, compacted. Why was that? What was happening?

"Did someone drive you here?" she asked.

Beth shook her head. "I've hired a car."

Stepping to the window, Harriet could see an aged-looking, pale-beige Wrangler now parked on the drive. It had only two seats and a carrying area in the rear, into which was neatly folded the Jeep's canvas roof. She turned back towards Beth, thankful that the darkness was masking her own expression.

"Why?"

"We've been hanging around here too long. I thought we'd just move on down the coast."

And Harriet was about to blurt out 'but we love Alsiso!' – when she realised that the two words 'but' and 'love' sat very heavily with her by now. She loved Beth. But what had she still gone and got up to?

The apartment complex was well lit, and she could see Beth's face quite clearly. And the look on it spoke volumes. It asked, 'Want to know where I've been all day? Should I enquire the same of you?'

Then it suddenly relaxed. The lazy, easy smile returned.

They went to bed and, as was usually the case, Beth attended first to Harriet. All of the familiar moves. All of the so-needed touches and caresses.

And yet … this time, Harriet could not stop thinking about what she'd done this afternoon. It left her stiff, uncomfortable again. Drained of all sensation once more.

In the end, as with Cody, she was forced to pretend something. The first time she had ever had to pretend that with Beth.

And once Beth was asleep? She curled into a tight, hard ball, and then gave herself over to quiet tears again. What had she *done*?

*

Come morning, Beth announced that she was going to scout ahead for them. Alone. She gave Harriet just the briefest of pecks on the cheek before she left, and looked pleased with herself as she sailed off in her new vehicle down the driveway.

She knew what had happened, Harriet now realised instinctually. She had either seen or guessed or found out somehow. It all seemed to be behind them now, though, never to be mentioned. The only thing she had to be quite sure of was that Cody understood.

He wasn't anywhere in sight when she walked into the courtyard of La Cocina. But Rodrigo was there, laying out fresh napkins, so she enquired after him.

Rodrigo just frowned unhappily. "He's gone. Lit out in the night without a word."

"Are you sure?"

"All his stuff's gone. And I paid him up till Friday too. Damned drifters."

The words kept turning over in Harriet's mind without settling properly. Gone? But he'd been talking, just yesterday, about doing certain 'things' in the future. And he didn't seem the type to turn tail and run just because she'd got annoyed with him.

She started to remember other things as well. The powerful sensation of being watched while she had been with him. The way that Beth had been gone the whole day. And the sudden, unannounced appearance of a vehicle with a load-carrying area and folded canvas in the rear.

For carrying what? Carrying it where?

An answer occurred to her that made her turn around and walk back out without another word.

*

It took her just under a quarter of an hour to reach the rocks. There was a heavy set of tyre tracks leading to and from them which had not been there a couple of days back.

Breathlessly, she made her way over the jagged grey surfaces, hunting for any tiny signs of something being dragged. There were none. She peered into some of the large, rough-edged tubes that led downwards. The ocean was churning at the bottom of them as usual, but she could make out nothing else down there.

She gazed out across the surface of the dark, unsettled water. A black triangular fin came into view for a few seconds, then just slipped away.

This was totally ridiculous. She was being even more insane than she had been yesterday. God, she thought of how big Cody was, and how small Beth, and her mind began to settle, her limbs started to relax. What she'd been imagining wasn't possible.

She was standing by now, on the flat section of rock they always lay on. Right beside the deep pool. So she looked down there.

Hermit crabs were scuttling across the stones, as always. Tiny fish flitted between the thick, undulating strands of weed.

One strand moved off to the side for a moment. Just long enough for Harriet to catch a glimpse of something shining. Something gold. It was gone again almost as soon as she had seen it.

She dropped to her knees, her heart thumping, waiting for the weed to move aside again. But now it didn't.

The rumble of an engine, then a crunch of tyres, announced the re-appearance of the Jeep. It stopped above her and Beth got out, still looking extremely pleased with herself. Shouted, "I thought I might find you here. What? Lost something? Looking for something?"

Harriet climbed back to her feet, trying to keep her expression blank. She could feel her sinews quivering gently as Beth came quickly down the slope towards her.

"What's that?"

"You looked like you were searching for something, that's all. Forget it." Reaching her, Beth planted a deep kiss on her mouth. "I've found the ideal place. A little fishing village about eight miles south.

I've already put money down on a room by the harbour. It's just perfect."

Well *that* was a relief at least. To be getting away from here.

"When are we going?"

"Tomorrow morning."

"Not today?"

Beth shook her head. "No way. Because today, my love, I want to lie here with you. Can't we do that? In this special place? Just lie here? One last time?"

Except that none of it was really a question. Because, the whole time she was asking it, Beth had rested her hands on Harriet's shoulders and was applying a gentle but firm pressure, not forcing her so much as gradually, inexorably easing her downwards.

And Harriet had never understood, until that moment, exactly how strong, physically, Beth was.

Usually, when they lay together in this place, it was side by side and on their backs, their shoulders almost, not quite, touching. But this time, for the first time, Beth wrapped her arms around Harriet tightly, and didn't even release her grip when she fell into a light, comfortable sleep.

Harriet lay there with her eyes wide open the whole while, but she remained entirely still, wondering what might happen if she dared to move.

Nine Rocks

"Incredible!"

John lets the word out as a quiet exhalation, gawping at the pale stone globes.

Meg smiles, as though taking his reaction for a personal compliment. She has got here a day ahead of him, and is feeling quite proprietorial by now.

"Tell you what's even more incredible? They're exactly the correct dimensions in relation to each other, every one of them. I measured them all."

"And how old, exactly?"

"If they were created at the same time as the painted symbols, which is reasonable to assume, then carbon dating gives the paint at somewhere around twenty three hundred B.C."

"More than four thousand years?" And now John whistles.

"Definitely pre-Hopi," Meg acknowledges. "What kind of culture could have done this?"

They are in a large cave of the same pale stone. The floor is grit and sand and dust, covered with Meg's footprints now and partially compacted. They have come down by means of a ladder which runs right up to the edge of a jagged hole in the ceiling. A beam of desert sunlight shines down almost on them, but mostly they are using torches. Shadows flicker all around them when they move.

In front of John on the gritty floor sit nine rocks which have been carved and polished into smooth balls, ranging in size from – first on the left – ping-pong sized to – the fifth one along – a beach-ball. The last, the ninth, is little too. They are arranged in a perfectly straight line; Meg has measured that as well. And what they seem to represent is wholly unbelievable.

Behind the nine rocks, painted on the uneven cave wall, are rows of primitive looking symbols, simple triangles and the like. This is what has brought John out here. Though they both hail out of C.U. Berkeley, Meg is an archaeologist, whereas John specialises in defunct and ancient languages.

*

When they first met, a year back, Meg was tense and sometimes hostile around John the first couple of months, to his bemusement. They later found out it was a cultural misunderstanding, she taking his British accent and his natural reticence for signs of snobbishness. She was laughingly apologetic when she found out how untrue that was, and made it up to him by taking him out for dinner. He didn't mind being asked, and she liked that in a man. They ended up in bed that same night.

*

"Only the gas giants were visible when they were first discovered," Meg explains now. "I only found the rest when I realised what they might be and started to dig."

Looking closer, John can see how the grit flooring has been cleared away round Mercury through to Mars, and then round Pluto.

"How exactly were they come across?"

"A couple of kids of quad-bikes. One of them jumps a bump – " she glances back up to the hole they have descended from, "and his front wheels come crashing through. He was lucky not to have fallen the whole way – that roof's pretty thin."

"But … how the hell'd a culture four thousand years old know about nine planets?"

"I'll tell you what's even weirder, pally. They're not perfect globes. They're slightly irregular at their upper axis, the same way the real planets are. And I'm willing to bet, when I finally get around to actually picking one up, the lower axis is the same."

John squints at the nine smooth rocks. "A hoax, then?"

"We'll know better when the big equipment turns up. But my gut instinct is – not."

"Then …?"

"The writing might explain things better. So get to it, lingo-dude."

John walks carefully around the row of stones and plays his torchlight on the large, faded inscriptions. His mouth purses and his brow creases uncomfortably.

"This can't be. This looks to me like a variant on early Phoenician."

"Really? Well, we're not too far from Phoenix."

"Ho-ho! Look, I mean the Phoenicians were great sailors and all, but I don't think they got quite this far. Besides which, this apparently pre-dates them."

"Mysteries of the ancients," Meg responds, still kidding him, still relaxed. "That's the business that we're in."

They both set to work. They are the advance party – the main team back at the university is still making preparations and will be here late tomorrow. So there is an urgency about the way that John and Meg work now. They want to have arrived at the main conclusions by the time the rest turn up. It will enhance their academic reputations. Besides which, they both know what a pleasurable drug triumphalism is.

John takes out a pen and pad and begins checking the symbols off against each other. Meg? She has a camera out by now, and is photographing the nine rocks from every conceivable angle. The big flash goes off constantly, throwing the cave into sharp relief. John doesn't mind it. Glances around at her every so often. She is wearing khaki shorts and Timberland boots, and he loves the sight of her bare, tanned legs poised at various angles.

They're both in their middle forties. John played rugby in his youth and is just over six foot and broad-shouldered, though his gut has gone a little soft these days and he has to wear glasses to watch TV. Meg, though she's a year older than him and five inches shorter, is naturally fit and likes, in her off-hours, to ride horses and climb rocks and swim, and has a wonderfully toned figure. She teases him about the love-handles, but actually likes them.

Like all people who enter a new relationship at their age, they bring a lot of baggage with them. Meg has been married twice, both times briefly, and has been in a long string of other relationships beyond that. She has a twenty-two year old daughter – Janine – who lives in New York these days. She has additionally had two affairs with women, and she's told John about that.

John only married late. He has an ex-wife and two children back in Oxford, the children being eight and six. He speaks to the kids on the phone every week, religiously, and flies back to England to visit them twice a year. Meg has not accompanied him as yet, though he's assured her that she will do when they're ready.

*

The language is remarkably similar to Phoenician, to John's bemusement. But that just makes it easier for him to translate. After some double-checking, he is ready.

"Got it," he announces.

Meg, who is growing tired of working with the camera, stops and looks up at him.

"Not bad."

"It's a prophecy."

"The winner of this year's Kentucky Derby, I can only hope?"

John shakes his head. "Somewhat more significant than that. It reads: 'This is how it was when the world started. This is how it shall be when the world comes to an end.'"

They both look at each other quizzically, since this item has been in the news for several weeks by now.

"When does that happen – do you remember?" John asks.

"I'm not sure." Meg goes very thoughtful for a moment. "But I know someone who will be sure. At NASA."

"NASA?"

"Professor Wes Cardew, no less. I dated him for a while."

"Is there anyone in the academic world you haven't dated?"

She grins. "Shut up, you."

She heads up the ladder and John follows her. The bright sunlight makes them squint when they emerge. A mild breeze is blowing, slightly off-setting the intense heat. This whole area of desert is, to John's eyes, a dried blood colour. There are patches of ochre and streaks of yellow, but brownish-red is the predominant colour. The rich green of the few shrubs and the sharp blue of the sky only emphasise that.

They head over to the camper van. Meg fishes around inside until she finds her address book, and then gets onto Houston on the satellite phone.

John hangs around outside while she exchanges pleasantries. She hasn't spoken to the guy in three years, after all.

In early autumn, they will head up to New England and they'll perhaps hire a boat. They've both sailed before and they both love that part of the States when fall approaches. John is already looking forward to it, and he thinks about it now.

Meg stops speaking on the phone and pokes her head out through the camper door.

"15:27 precisely, tomorrow. Perfect alignment of the solar system."

"Have you made a will?"

"Knock it off."

They both walk back to the hole and peer through it, but don't go down again.

"Doesn't it strike you as a big co-incidence?" Meg asks. "That this thing was discovered just a bare couple of days before the planets actually align?"

"I still think it's a hoax."

Shadows are starting to lengthen by this time. They don't want to be in the cave when it gets dark. So Meg retrieves her camera, then they head back to the camper and undress and shower together. John stands closely behind Meg, soaping her breasts and the down between her thighs.

"It couldn't happen anyway, could it?" he asks as his hands move.

"What?"

"The world suddenly ending? I mean, nuclear winter would take a while. A worldkiller asteroid would be fairly fast but not immediate."

She closes one of her hands over each of his, and groans a moment. Then murmurs, "There is one way."

"Really?"

"Really. When a star goes supernova, it throws out massive amounts of gamma radiation over a long distance. If we got into the path of that, it would be all over, for every living creature on this planet, in mere seconds."

"You are kidding me?"

"I'm not. Apparently, our solar system has been moving through a fairly safe part of the galaxy the past few thousand years. But we're now moving into a region where it's far more likely." She turns round to face him and begins to kiss his chest. "And gamma radiation moves at the precise same speed as light. Which means we wouldn't even see it coming. Which is more than I can say for you."

They don't even bother to dry themselves off. Just struggle out of the shower and slam down on the bed. It is a heated act, mostly penetrative at first, and John climaxes quickly. After that though, they become more languorous, explorative, John using his fingers and tongue until Meg is fully satisfied.

When she finally gets up, there's that special lightness to her movements. She pulls back on just her underwear and shirt, and then sets about dinner. She's a terrific cook, and makes for them a stew of pork and haricot beans to her own recipe. They set up a folding table and two camp chairs and eat in the open. Afterwards, John goes back inside and returns with two glasses and a bottle of well-chilled Napa Valley rosé.

It is fully dark by now. Thousands of stars gleam overhead. A tiny gleaming chip, no larger than a dust mote, sails above them – a man-made satellite, catching the harsh brightness of the absentee sun.

"We're actually sitting on a great big ball of rock which itself is speeding through a warmthless vacuum," John says, thinking about the objects in the cave again. "I know that's the truth, but I can never quite get my head around it."

Meg lights one of the two cigarettes she allows herself each day. "Tell you what I find weird? When I was younger, I used to see life as an unbroken stream of ambition, advancement, opportunity, and I genuinely believed it was that which would fulfil me. These days? All that really counts are moments like these. I think Sartre called them 'blue moments'? Little chunks of time when everything is perfect, everything just gels and levels out, and you're fully conscious of the fact that you are happy."

She thinks about the prophecy again, then adds, "I sometimes find myself wondering how many more I'll be allowed before my time is up."

John gazes at her evenly. "That's like in 'The Sheltering Sky'. We only get to see a limited number of full moons in a lifetime."

"Never did care for that book. Too cold." She smiles at him, knowing that he disagrees. It is one of his favourite novels. "If it were tomorrow? If it were all to end?"

"It's not going to," John says. "You're being morbid."

Meg looks back up at the sky, and her gaze becomes distant. "No," she mutters. "I'm not sure at all that's the correct word."

*

Both of them have secrets. John's? He actually has a third child back in England, though he's never seen it, doesn't know its name or even its gender. He had a brief fling with a waitress when he was in his late twenties. She fell pregnant, decided to raise the child on her own, and left Oxford a few weeks later – he never found out where she disappeared to. Sometimes he wonders what the child looks like.

He's meant to tell Meg several times but, for some strange reason, he feels embarrassed about the whole incident, as though it has left a stain on his character. He has resolved by now though, that he will tell her, will force himself, before the end of the year.

For her own part Meg, back when she was nineteen years of age, was raped while very drunk by a boy she knew after a party at her college. She cannot even remember many details, just the queasy sensation of lying like a rag-doll, unable to do anything about the fact she was in pain. She never reported it, and learned after a few years how to push it to the far recesses of her thoughts.

She is still unsure whether to tell John or not. She can't see for the life of her what earthly good it would do, but she hates keeping anything from him.

*

The next day they sleep especially late, taking advantage of their last few hours of freedom before the rest of the team arrive, and only get back down into the cave just after noon.

John studies the writing again, trying to understand how it could possibly be so much like a language from North Africa. Meg circles the nine rocks like a waiting, curious shark.

She finally makes up her mind. "Well, here goes." And she crosses to the smallest of them, Mercury.

"Let's see what this baby looks like underneath."

She bends to pick it up. But cannot seem to. Her whole body jerks a moment. Then she looks thoroughly mystified.

"What the hell ...? It won't budge."

Under John's gaze, she starts to clear more grit away from the base of the little globe, first with a large brush then, as the solution becomes more apparent, with her hands. Finally, she's scooping double-handfuls of the stuff.

"What the hell ...?"

Her shout brings John hurrying over. She is on her knees and gazing up at him, her normally brown face gone pale.

Are his eyes playing tricks on him? John crouches down to get a better look.

He's startled too. It is not simply a free-standing globe that they've been looking at all this time. It terminates with a thin, downward-leading stem, all carved from the same piece of stone.

"Help me," Meg demands.

They keep on digging with their hands until they reach the true floor of the cave, some twenty inches further down. The stem emerges from it, but not by attachment. It is actually part of it.

"This is crazy!"

They start on the next, Venus, to find the same is true. Then Earth.

Meg is actually shaking by this juncture. She goes hurrying back up the ladder, and re-appears a minute later clutching a hand-held vacuum. She crosses to the largest globe, Jupiter, and begins to clear the grit away from that, working diligently with the hose, having to empty the cylinder in the cave's dark corner several times.

When she is finally done, she measures the distance from the top of the globe to the actual stone floor.

"Thirty eight inches."

Then, to be entirely sure, she moves right away from the nine globes and digs another hole. Once done, once fully certain of her suspicions, she stares at John with actual shock.

"The same. Do you know what this means? Whoever made the globes didn't carve them out of free-standing rock. They lowered the whole floor of the cave by thirty eight inches. That's an incredible task."

"And most likely proves the whole thing is a hoax," John says.

"No, I don't think so." She ushers him over, and plays her torch down the last hole she has dug. "See those chisel markings, yes? I see them all the time. They were made by ancient tools, not modern steel ones."

They stare at each other, their minds reeling at the awesomeness of what they have uncovered.

"I'd better inform the team," Meg says at last, quite numbly.

She goes back up the ladder, again to use the satellite phone. John remains where he is, gazing round as though he has found himself on a completely different planet.

*

They both like jazz and modern art. They both support the Democrats. They love movies. Both of them got the point of 'Mulholland Drive' – they caught it long after its first release at a re-showing in an art-house theatre – while most of the rest of the audience were filing out shaking their heads.

Meg has a secret passion for daytime soaps, which John finds ridiculous. John, a few months after moving to the States, began developing a liking for baseball and Meg – having ignored her national sport her entire life – got interested too once she started going out with him. They've been to two Giants games already this year, driving into San Francisco specially for the occasion.

They both like all kinds of food, especially Japanese and Greek. Oh, and Italian. And Thai. Meg will get hold of some dope occasionally, which they will smoke at home together.

John enjoys South Park a lot, but the humour doesn't appeal to Meg. Neither of them are interested in status symbols of the flashy car/gold watch variety, though Meg likes good clothes when she's not working.

The fact that they both abhor fast-food doesn't mean they never eat it.

Janine's birth was so difficult that Meg was rendered unable to have another child. She's told John that too.

They keep thinking 'fall's a long way off still – maybe we'll take an earlier, short trip before the big one to New England'. And they both keep wondering where.

*

When Meg doesn't return after half an hour, John heads for the roof himself, to see where she has got to.

She is crouching on the ground a few yards from the hole, with her back to him. Doesn't even seem to notice he is there. As he starts to quietly walk around her, he can see that there are four cigarette butts mashed out on the soil next to her boots. She is gazing into the far distance with a tense, thoughtful expression on her narrow face.

"Did you tell them?" he asks.

She jerks, then peers up at him, slightly blinded by the sun. She nods.

"And ... what reaction?"

"Amazement. They can't wait to get here."

"So what's up?"

Meg peers off into the distance once again.

"If it was ancients who did that ... do you realise how much work it must have entailed for them? So many years? So much effort? And you know what that suggests to me?"

John waits for her answer.

"That they were entirely serious. It made me think, that's all. What if last night were it, the last? My final 'blue moment'?"

John crouches down behind her and starts to massage her bare, smooth shoulders. He is grinning, and it seeps into his voice. "The world isn't going to end at 3:27 this afternoon."

"I have your word on that?"

"Absolutely."

John thinks about New England again. Yes, they'll definitely hire a boat. He imagines them sprawled out on the deck, their arms around each other.

*

Even he is slightly tense, though, by the time the hour approaches. Their movements become slower and they talk less. Meg keeps glancing at her watch. They have been assessing, up till now, the amount of work the team will have to do to clear out all the grit and dust and reveal the whole structure. A lot of work. But entirely worth it.

"Three twenty six," John announces, holding up his wrist. "Here goes."

He still has a grin on his face, but it is now faintly nervous. Meg looks drawn and apprehensive all over again. They are standing at the far ends of the row of polished stones, facing each other, and the dimness of the cavern bleeds away the edges of their bodies.

When their watch dials move to twenty seven, they both hold their breaths for a long moment, then exhale. Meg even lets out a tiny gasp. Which echoes.

Then John's grin becomes a genuine one again. He spreads his hands.

"Still here!"

*

Maybe Hawaii. Hawaii would be nice for a short break. Or Cancun.

*

They head back up the ladder, glad to leave the cave by now. The desert is still brownish red, the sky still a piercing blue, the breeze still blowing. Their fingers entwine gently as they stroll back, side by side, towards the camper van.

A lizard appears on top of a rock a moment, and then darts away. A kite wheels overhead.

Meg and John are smiling, as though they have just shared some intimately private joke, albeit one which they have been the butt of.

'No, definitely Hawaii', John decides.

Meg? She begins wondering how long all nine planets remain perfectly aligned. A few minutes, surely?

The breeze suddenly transforms to a gust of wind, blowing up dust, making the shrubs around them rattle.

Meg stops as that happens, a frown creasing her forehead and her lips tightening briskly. Her head lifts as though she has caught a strange scent on the heated air.

She turns to John and asks him, "Hey, can you feel someth

'At any moment the rip can occur, the edges fly back, and the giant maw will be revealed.'
Paul Bowles – THE SHELTERING SKY.

More quality fiction from Elastic Press

☐	The Virtual Menagerie	Andrew Hook	SOLD OUT
☐	Open The Box	Andrew Humphrey	£3.00
☐	Second Contact	Gary Couzens	£5.00
☐	Sleepwalkers	Marion Arnott	SOLD OUT
☐	Milo & I	Antony Mann	SOLD OUT
☐	The Alsiso Project	Edited by Andrew Hook	SOLD OUT
☐	Jung's People	Kay Green	SOLD OUT
☐	The Sound of White Ants	Brian Howell	£5.00
☐	Somnambulists	Allen Ashley	SOLD OUT
☐	Angel Road	Steven Savile	SOLD OUT
☐	Visits to the Flea Circus	Nick Jackson	£5.00
☐	The Elastic Book of Numbers	Edited by Allen Ashley	SOLD OUT
☐	The Life To Come	Tim Lees	SOLD OUT
☐	Trailer Park Fairy Tales	Matt Dinniman	SOLD OUT
☐	The English Soil Society	Tim Nickels	£5.99
☐	The Last Days of Johnny North	David Swann	£6.99
☐	The Ephemera	Neil Williamson	£5.99
☐	Unbecoming	Mike O'Driscoll	£6.99
☐	Photocopies of Heaven	Maurice Suckling	£5.99
☐	Extended Play	Edited by Gary Couzens	£6.99
☐	So Far, So Near	Mat Coward	£5.99
☐	Going Back	Tony Richards	£5.99

All these books are available at your local bookshop or can be ordered direct from the publisher. Indicate the number of copies required and fill in the form below.

Name_____

(Block letters please)

Address_____

Send to Elastic Press, 85 Gertrude Road, Norwich, Norfolk, NR3 4SG.
Please enclose remittance to the value of the cover price plus: £1.50 for the first book plus 50p per copy for each additional book ordered to cover postage and packing. Applicable in the UK only.

While every effort is made to keep prices low, it is sometimes necessary to increase prices at short notice. Elastic Press reserve the right to show on covers and charge new retail prices which may differ from those advertised in the text or elsewhere.

Want to be kept informed? Keep up to date with Elastic Press titles by writing to the above address, or by visiting www.elasticpress.com and adding your email details to our online mailing list.

Elastic Press: Winner of the British Fantasy Society Best Small Press award 2005

Extended Play:
The Elastic Book of Music

What does music do for you? Is it an art form, mood enhancer, or just something to jump around to? From the orchestra pit to the mosh pit music inspires our lives, is universal and personal, futuristic yet primordial. As the soundtrack trigger to a thousand memories it can be seductive yet soulful, energetic and prophetic. But the immediacy of music has rarely been exploited within literature. Until now...

With fiction from Marion Arnott, Becky Done, Andrew Humphrey, Emma Lee, Tim Nickels, Rosanne Rabinowitz, Philip Raines, Tony Richards, Nels Stanley, and Harvey Welles.

Accompanying the stories, songwriters comment on how fiction has influenced their music, with contributions from JJ Burnel, Gary Lightbody, Chris Stein, Sean "Grasshopper Mackowiak, Lene Lovich, Chris T-T, Rebekah Delgado, Tall Poppies, jof owen, and Iain Ross.

www.elasticpress.com